Between
THE
Lighthouse
AND
You

Between THE Lighthouse AND you

Michelle Lee

FARRAR STRAUS GIROUX
NEW YORK

Farrar Straus Giroux Books for Young Readers
An imprint of Macmillan Children's Publishing Group, LLC
120 Broadway, New York, NY 10271 • mackids.com

Printed in the United States of America by
LSC Communications, Harrisonburg, Virginia
Book design by Trisha Previte
Title page and part opener illustrations by Dion MBD
Dedication and chapter title illustrations by Trisha Previte
First edition, 2022

1   3   5   7   9   10   8   6   4   2

Library of Congress Cataloging-in-Publication Data
Names: Lee, Michelle (Michelle S.), author.
Title: Between the lighthouse and you / Michelle Lee.
Description: First edition. | New York: Farrar Straus Giroux Books for
Young Readers, 2022. | Audience: Ages 8–12. | Audience: Grades 4–6. |
Summary: With her family, twelve-year-old Alice Jones visits Aviles Island,
where her mother disappeared long ago, and forms an unlikely friendship
with Leo Mercury, who also wants to use the island's special power to
contact a lost loved one.
Identifiers: LCCN 2020047109 | ISBN 978-0-374-31450-7 (hardback)
Subjects: CYAC: Missing persons—Fiction. | Supernatural—Fiction. |
Friendship—Fiction. | Family life—Fiction. |
Islands—Florida—Fiction. | Florida—Fiction.
Classification: LCC PZ7.1.L4242 Bet 2021 | DDC [Fic]—dc23

LC record available at https://lccn.loc.gov/2020047109

Our books may be purchased in bulk for promotional, educational, or
business use. Please contact your local bookseller or the Macmillan Corporate
and Premium Sales Department at (800) 221-7945 ext. 5442 or by email at
MacmillanSpecialMarkets@macmillan.com.

For my dad, Richard Stoddard.
Please send me good tidings from wherever you are.
I love you.

Alice

It's All in My Head

I can't talk.

I open my mouth and nothing comes out.

It happens year-round, typically when I plan to get on some sort of boat, even the clunky kind you pedal around small lakes for fifteen bucks an hour. But now it's April. The anniversary of my mother's funeral.

There's no telling how long it will last. This is Day 2. I'm at Dr. Figg's with my dad. Dr. Figg's office is beige and windowless, like it doesn't have a voice either.

Dad checks us in with the receptionist as I settle into one of the tan plastic chairs. Dr. Figg will look in my mouth. She'll look up my nose. She'll stick a thing in my ears. She'll *hmmm* and *ahhh*. She'll ask me to scribble stuff down. She'll eventually say to my father (because I'm a kid, and the state of my throat obviously hinders my hearing and ability to understand):

"As you know, I believe it's psychosomatic, and her voice

will return whenever it's ready, but Alice could try an anti-histamine, saline gargling, or even some breathing exercises." *Psychosomatic.* A big word for *It's all in your head.* I looked it up a long time ago.

When this started, I was six and Dad panicked. Took me to four different pediatricians and three different counselors—child, grief, family—even a local pastor who smelled like old books and oatmeal cookies.

They said kindly, in one fashion or another: "Give it time. It's her body's way of dealing with her mother's tragic and sudden passing."

Passing. As if Mom just dissolved and went somewhere else. Easily. No unexpected storm. No sailing accident. No empty boat found. No Mom missing.

Dad still worries, still takes me in for a checkup when I go silent. Every time. And every time, Dr. Figg smiles at me like she's hoping for a light-bulb moment. Besides the routine examination, she usually asks me a bunch of questions and makes me free-write my answers. Free-write my feelings. Mostly about my family. My dad. My younger sister, Clara. My dad's . . . girlfriend?

I still don't know what to call her after three and a half years.

Neesha Hamilton. Neesha.

Occasionally, Dr. Figg asks me to write about Mom, who disappeared-drowned-died-insert-similar-verb-here. Only I believe she's still out there. But I can't say that at home. The first time I tried, I was littler. At Mom's funeral. My dad got upset. So did Clara, who was two and confused about where Mom went. Even now, they freeze up when I mention the possibility.

Early on, Dr. Figg would ask: *Why do you think you lose your voice, Alice?*

And I would write in angry crayon letters: *Mom's not gone.*

Sessions with Dr. Figg don't really help, but I come anyway because of the sad wrinkle in Dad's forehead that lasts as long as my silence does. And, strangely, because losing my voice reminds me that, even if no one wants to hear me, I have hope.

"Doc's a few minutes behind," Dad says. At nearly six foot three, he fills the seat next to me, and his legs sprawl in front of him. He reaches into the roomy pocket of his khaki pants and pulls out a small book with a leathery, rose-colored cover. Dad's constantly reading or taking notes for his job as the host of his own radio show, *Our Town with Oliver Jones*, which airs on our local public station. Though most of his work gets done on his phone, he's a fan of real books.

To my surprise, he holds the book out to me. "Thought you might like to have this while we wait."

I shoot him a look that I've perfected during voiceless days, basically a combination of *Why?* and *Say more.*

"It's another one of your mom's journals. I found it in the basement last night when I went to fix the water heater. Stuff fell out of some boxes when I moved them out of the way. Since you've become the official caretaker of her library, I thought you'd want it."

I nod vigorously and mouth the words *Thank you*, as big as I can make them. Even if I had my voice, I honestly don't know if I could speak. My heart is skipping. A journal of Mom's that I've never seen or read before.

She was a cultural anthropologist, basically A NORMAL SCI-ENTIST, BUT WAY COOLER, according to the painted wooden sign that used to hang above her desk. But if anyone asked, she'd say she studied people and how they live. In reality, she studied people and how they could communicate with the dead. Or maybe the not-quite-dead, as she sometimes said.

Before she disappeared, our living room overflowed with her textbooks, notebooks, and binders, not to mention paperbacks by the dozens. After the accident, little by little, I squirreled everything away into my room, which Dad and Clara didn't seem to mind. At six, I couldn't read much, and what I could read I didn't understand, but I wanted to. Clues to where Mom had gone had to be in there. Now, at twelve, I'm not much farther along in connecting the dots between her millions of words. At the same time, they are the only chance I have at finding answers.

I open the journal's soft cover. Mom titled the first page *Special Collections*, with a list of books and call numbers underneath in black ink. The next few pages are the same. I hate to even think it, but I'm disappointed. After all, as much as I love seeing Mom's handwriting, what she wrote is pretty boring.

Wait.

The lists give way to a page of question marks in dark pencil, like she'd traced them several times. The way I do when I'm thinking hard. Then—

Happy accident! Found a letter someone obviously forgot, stuck to the inside cover of an old Florida atlas. Brittle, water-stained, can't read the names, but compelling. Aviles Island—can people there send actual messages to and from those who have passed away? Once a year? The writer called them "tidings." So, news from the beyond? Need to follow the trail.

I reread the paragraph. Aviles Island. That's where my mom was doing her research when she didn't come back. Was this the spark that led her there? Did Mom follow the trail and discover she was right somehow? What if she's out there, wanting to prove she's not completely . . . gone? Wanting to send *us* a message? What if we have to be on that island to get it?

There's more writing in the margin, slanting vertically in different ink as if Mom wrote it on another day.

Ran into Dr. Ingram in the hallway. We chatted about our work, and I told him about the letter I found. He was surprised since, it turns out, he had a serious relationship in college with someone from Aviles Island. She told him about their tradition of sending messages to family members who died. But they broke up before he got to visit the island. Never spoke to her again, never gave her story much thought. Still skeptical! But too much is adding up. Must talk to someone from Aviles to corroborate.

Dad goes back up to the receptionist's desk to do something with our insurance. When he returns, I point to the pen in his pocket and flip to a blank page in my mom's journal.

When he hands me the pen, I scribble: *What do you know about Aviles Island? Mom's research about the tidings?*

He blinks at the questions. I can tell he's choosing his words carefully. They're being edited deep in his brown eyes. "Not much. Is that what she wrote about in the journal?"

More scribble. *We have to go to Aviles Island. To see if what she thought is right.*

Dad's expression softens. "I've been to the island, honey. Years ago. To help look for your mom. There's nothing there."

Did you ever talk to Mom about how the tidings worked? Did you ever try to send her a message?

"No, I didn't." Dad strains to keep his voice even, and I know I'm pushing. But I can't stop. "Searching for your mother was serious, Alice."

Mom's research was serious. What if we need to go back to the island so she can contact us?

Dad sighs, gazing off toward the receptionist's desk as if willing our names to be called. I'm not surprised by his reaction. He loved my mom, but was never too keen on her work. I remember their low-voice conversations about how she was forever seeking out tiny dots on the map, chasing myths that took her far away from us. After Mom's disappearance, he gave me some scientific articles to read about death. So I could reason everything out.

"I had people trolling that ocean for nearly a year," he says finally, his eyes glistening. "No message in a bottle will bring your mom back to us."

I scrawl. *It might.*

"Alice Jones?"

Dad stands when Dr. Figg calls from the doorway. I can tell he's relieved to escape my questions and make small talk instead, because there's nothing small about this. At Mom's funeral, Dad, Clara, my dad's family, my mom's family, my mom's colleagues from her university, her friends—they all cried and cried. But I couldn't. It was like I could hear my mom saying, "Well, this isn't right," the way she did every time something was going terribly wrong, with a little bit of hope brightening each word. I haven't cried about anything since. I know Mom has to be in that in-between place.

Dr. Figg huddles with Dad, but motions for me to go back to her office, where there's more beige. First, she'll have me write about subjects I like in school—English and social studies. Then about how Clara and I are getting along—on a good day, scale of 1 to 5, we might be at a 2½ to 3. Finally, *my future goals*. Right now, I have only one: get to Aviles Island and send Mom a message.

So after Dad's safe in the waiting room again, and Dr. Figg pulls out the chair across from me and hands me a pencil and paper and tells me to jot down how I'm feeling today, I write: *If you got the chance to talk to someone you'd lost, would you take it?*

Alice

One Small Shred

Dad plays news radio on the short drive home, which keeps him from talking. It's okay, because the whole me-scribbling-an-answer thing when we're in the car is tricky anyway. Besides, I'm anxious to get home. I have a mountain of my mom's papers to sort through. It's a long shot to think I can find something related to the tidings or Aviles Island before dinner, but at least I can start the search.

I'm out of the car the second Dad and I pull in front of the house. Neesha calls a cheery hello from the desk in the corner of the kitchen where she's doing work on her laptop. I wave, but stay on course. I feel a little rude heading straight to my room, since she routinely makes a point to check in with me, even the times when my "voice" is chicken-scratch penciled across paper.

Neesha and my dad met when he was "not ready to date." Shaving and showering were pretty much becoming foreign ideas. I was eight and a half and not looking for a new mom, but she was nice and treated Clara and me like kids who didn't need a new mom. Neesha is as short and curvy as my dad is tall and solid. Neesha lives with us most days, though she has her own apartment an hour away in D.C., where she's an orthopedist. She persuades Dad to eat salad—the green kind, not just the potato or chicken kind. She encourages Dad to stop wearing the same shirt three days in a row. She packs Dad a lunch, plus makes them for me and Clara, too. And she has us talk at dinner about our days and about the world. Sometimes Neesha prays and goes to church, and I've asked her things about God, but she told me everyone should find things out for themselves, find out what they believe. Neesha also knows about Mom and how she disappeared.

As I enter my room and shut the door, I wonder if I should show her Mom's journal later. Get her thoughts on all this. For now, I'm toeing off my sneakers, setting Mom's journal on my nightstand, and wedging myself into the impressive mountain range of folders, manila envelopes, binders, and spiral notebooks that make a low wall between my bed and closet. Somewhere in all of it, there has to be one small shred about Aviles Island that will get me closer to finding Mom.

I start sorting, flipping, skimming. Not that one . . . Not that one . . . Something, anything?

The rejection pile by my elbow gets bigger and shakier. When I set a blue three-ring binder on top, the whole thing falls Jenga-style, knocking into other towers and sending paper everywhere.

Frustration makes my chest burn and my eyes tingle. I

stare at the mass of Mom's writing, wishing she was more organized, wishing I was more organized, wishing I could blink and find exactly what I'm looking for. I've been searching through this stuff for years with no luck.

Curling my knees up against my body, I glance over at the big-face selfie of Toddler Me and Mom taped to the dry-erase board behind my door. Her cheesy smile makes me smile back every time. I can't let her down. It'll be worth it when I'm right. When she's right.

Better keep going.

I start gathering and aligning and restacking. A flimsy white envelope catches on the coil of a spiral notebook, and I shake it loose. It hits the floor, address-side up.

To Anny Jones. From John Mercury, the Lighthouse, Aviles Island.

Aviles Island. I can't believe this!

Amazed that I found something and nearly bursting with excitement, I open the envelope as carefully as I can and take out the note inside.

DEAR MS. JONES,

YOU ARE DEFINITELY PERSISTENT. BUT EVEN AFTER WHAT YOU SAID IN YOUR LAST LETTER, I HAVE SERIOUS RESERVATIONS ABOUT YOU VISITING THE ISLAND.

WE'RE A SMALL COMMUNITY. ALTHOUGH WE HAVE INCORPORATED SOME CREATURE COMFORTS WITH THE TIMES, WE HAVE TRIED TO KEEP OUR ENVIRONMENT RELATIVELY

UNSPOILED. THERE ARE NO REAL AMENITIES OR SERVICES TO ACCOMMODATE ANYTHING BUT THE OCCASIONAL TOURIST.

AS THE AVILES ISLAND LIGHTHOUSE KEEPER FOR MOST OF MY LIFE, BORN FROM A LINE OF LIGHTHOUSE KEEPERS, I DON'T WANT OUR TRADITIONS UNEARTHED AND UPENDED. FOLKS MIGHT GET FALSE HOPE, MIGHT NOT UNDERSTAND, OR WORSE YET, MIGHT WANT TO PUT US UNDER A MICROSCOPE. THE TIDINGS ARE SPECIAL TO US, WHICH IS WHY WE ONLY CELEBRATE THEM FOR A FEW DAYS EVERY JULY, TO MARK THE HISTORY OF WHEN THEY FIRST CAME. OUR HISTORY.

HOWEVER, I PRIDE MYSELF ON BEING AN EXCELLENT JUDGE OF CHARACTER, AND YOUR INTEREST AND INTENTIONS DO SEEM TRUE. DON'T GET TOO EXCITED—I REMAIN RELUCTANT. YET I HAVE DECIDED TO MEET WITH YOU, IF YOU VOW TO KEEP THINGS MUM. I DON'T WANT THE EASTERN SEABOARD FOLLOWING YOU DOWN HERE.

IF YOU SEND ME THE TIME OF YOUR ARRIVAL, I WILL ARRANGE A BOAT TO PICK YOU UP FROM THE MAINLAND, AS WELL AS YOUR LODGING. SEE YOU IN A FEW WEEKS.

SINCERELY,
JOHN MERCURY

If I could squeal, I totally would. Mom talked to this John Mercury about the tidings before she went to the island. He can help me send a message. This is it!

I pump the air a few times and groove out my happiness. Then reality slams into me. How can I convince Dad we need to go to Aviles Island, especially after our "conversation" at Dr. Figg's? Plus, Mom must've told Dad about John Mercury. After all, he was the reason she was going.

I hear my sister's voice down the hall, probably talking to Dad or Neesha. I'd ask Clara for help, but she's eight, and favors from her usually require endless negotiation. Last time I asked her to switch my garbage duty for her dishwashing, she wouldn't budge until I agreed to play this game called Pop! the Pig for a week straight. Dad tried explaining that Clara only wants to spend time with me, and I secretly like feeding the plastic pig cheeseburgers and watching his tummy grow, but sometimes Clara cheats, which leads to arguments that neither one of us wins.

More to the point, Clara has her own version of mute when I mention Mom or use the word *dead*.

"Alice?" Neesha calls through my closed door. "Thought you might like some hot chocolate after Dr. Figg's. Working through feelings definitely warrants some sugar."

Before I can make my way over, she opens the door cautiously. Her expression is bright but tentative, like she doesn't want to crash a party she's been formally invited to.

Neesha.

Neesha. *Of course.* She'll help me.

Tucking John Mercury's letter in the waist of my jeans, I mime for her to make herself comfortable on my bed. Then I grab Mom's journal from the nightstand and make my way over to the dry-erase board.

I need your help with something, I write in purple marker.

Neesha nods. "If I can."

We need to go to Aviles Island. In July. I give her Mom's journal, flipped to the page with the question marks. *Mom wrote this.*

Neesha begins to read. After waiting a few seconds, I hand her the letter from John Mercury.

I bounce on my toes impatiently as she takes that in, too. She looks from letter to journal, letter to journal, until her dark eyes become misty and her mouth falls open in slow understanding.

I write: *I want to send a message. A tiding to my mother.*

"You want to . . . wow, baby girl," Neesha murmurs, using a phrase usually reserved for Clara and not me because I'm twelve and almost a teenager, plus Neesha's the only mom Clara remembers. Clara even calls her Mom sometimes, which always catches me off guard. It makes my stomach feel good and bad, mixed-up and churny. "Did you show these to your dad?"

The dry-erase board is filling with my handwriting. I erase what I've written and start again. *I tried. Dad won't listen. But we have to go.*

"Alice."

There's sympathy in the way she says my name. She's been with us long enough to know my dad doesn't like to dwell on the past. So I write: *Please.*

She sighs and smiles kindly. "I admire you so much for never giving up hope."

I write more. *But it's more than hope now, right?*

Neesha studies the question-mark page in Mom's journal for a long moment. "The idea that someone could keep in touch with those who have passed—if it's true—is beyond incredible. Even so, this should be a conversation between you and your dad and Clara."

One last shot: *Help me convince them.*

"That's a mighty big ask," she says gently. "This wouldn't be a vacation."

But it's for our family.

"I'll think about it. I promise." Neesha lays the journal and letter down on the bedspread and stands. Before she opens the door, she wraps her arms around me. The soft curve of her body is more comforting than enthusiastic. But it boosts my sense of hope.

Alice

The Mighty Big Ask

For the rest of the afternoon, I can't concentrate. Forget the hot chocolate. Forget the homework. Forget anything but scouring the rest of my mom's journal and tearing through more of her papers for more details. Nothing else comes up.

"Anyone want dinner?" Dad announces from somewhere near the kitchen. I glance at my purple digital clock on the nightstand. Six fifteen.

Bug-eyed from reading so much, I drag my way to the front of the house. Halfway down the hall, I definitely smell pizza. Meatball pizza. Dad's ultimate go-to.

He's humming his happy food song and helping himself to a big slice when I get to the table. Definitely in a good mood.

As I slide into my chair next to Clara, Neesha catches my eye from across the table and smiles. Hmm. Did she arrange pizza night because my dad is known to say yes to anything after a meatball pie? Monopoly, early-morning bike rides, extra spending money? Possible road trip south this summer?

There's a few minutes of passing around salad, water, and Parmesan cheese, followed by a few minutes of Clara chatting about her after-school running club. Then Neesha says, "Alice showed me the pretty journal you gave her, Oliver."

"What journal?" Clara pipes up while Dad raises an eyebrow in surprise.

Happy food song over.

"I found a journal that belonged to your mother," Dad says nonchalantly.

"Oh." Clara's face falls. "Never mind."

Never mind. That's her deal when it comes to Mom. Every time I ask her if she remembers something—how Mom snorted when she laughed too hard, or how she wore these khaki pants that had a hundred pockets, one always filled with caramels in gold wrappers, or the snowy day when she made sleds out of garbage can lids so Clara and I could slide down the driveway—Clara immediately says no. Then she changes the subject. She never wants Mom on her mind.

"I never knew much about her research," Neesha says lightly. "But the tidings sound pretty compelling."

"Mm-hmm." Dad studies me pointedly over his pizza as he takes a bite.

"What are the tidings?" Clara asks.

Neesha goes on. "I wonder if Aviles Island would be an interesting topic for your radio show."

Dad's radio show? That's a great idea.

"My radio show?" Dad nearly chokes. "Are you serious?"

"I know you've only focused on small Maryland towns

with *Our Town*," Neesha answers with this blend of patience and ease only she possesses. "The rodeo grandmas in Union Bridge. That Baltimore family who has lived in the public library for more than a century. The Fort Washington wrestler who became a cupcake baker with his daughter. You have said you wanted to branch out. Your listeners might be fascinated by how residents on a small island on the Florida coast can get messages from those who have died. Could be a special edition?"

"An island in Florida?" Clara's waving her pizza. "As in theme parks, beaches, and . . . vacation?"

Obviously, she only heard the part she wanted to hear. Not to mention perfect change of subject. Time for me to jump in.

I dart out of my seat and snag a marker and pad of lined paper from a drawer. I scratch and dash—then hold up the paper like a sign:

Yes—vacation. We could go in July. Ask the people on Aviles Island how to contact Mom.

"My show isn't fantasy." Dad puts down his crust. "I can understand being intrigued by something your mom wrote, but there's no use chasing the impossible."

Mom didn't think so, I scrawl. *That's why she went.*

"Do we have to talk about this?" Clara mutters into her plate. "Or in Alice's case, *not* talk about this?"

I sneer at Clara, who sticks her tongue out at me.

"Okay," Neesha says, "maybe we should put a pin in this for now."

She looks at Dad, clearly wanting to smooth over the

tension, tension that is my fault. But I can't lose her idea. I write again.

You know Mom was going to talk with someone on the island, Dad. Imagine the hard-hitting questions you could ask.

Dad stares at the piece of paper in my hand, now crammed with handwritten scribble. His face is soft and sad around the edges.

"Oh, Ali, I wish you could let this go."

Ali.

Dad doesn't call me that often. Sometimes when he forgets that I'm big enough to tuck myself into bed and bunches me way down snug in my comforter. Sometimes when I have a sore throat and am stuck at home with chicken soup and TV. Soft-spot Dad. Snuggle-up Dad. Before-Mom-disappeared Dad.

"If you want to branch out, Dad, how about California instead?" Clara suggests. "There are beaches and theme parks there, too."

I glare at her. New subject, and chances are, one last-ditch effort. I write: *I will let this go, Dad. If we take a trip to Aviles Island and I don't get an answer from her.*

To my surprise, Dad doesn't shoot me down. He just takes a long drink of water.

"Nothing needs to be decided this minute, especially if the tidings tradition has been going on for several decades." Neesha slides me a small smile. "But this definitely inspires some thought about taking a family trip."

I smile back at her. Neesha's definitely more than my dad's girlfriend. In fact, the only thing terribly wrong with Neesha is that she's simply not my mother. Who is not dead. So I come up behind her and loop my arms around her shoulders. Out of my mouth, into her thick curly hair, falls a soundless *thank you.*

Alice
Family Meeting

I plump the bed pillows higher behind my back and crook my dinged-up laptop more securely in the V of my stomach and folded legs. John Mercury stares back at me from a black-and-white photo online, bearded and sturdy in the shadow of a tall, stately lighthouse.

It's been a week since our family discussion at dinner about Aviles Island, and I've come back to this website at least fifty times. The information's just basic stuff about when the lighthouse was built (1902) and about the general importance of lighthouses. There's a phone number, too. No email. Nothing about the tidings. I've gone down the rabbit hole of searches. The only thing I found were the same photos of grassy sand dunes over and over.

Now that my voice is back, I've thought about calling Mr. Mercury, but after my mom's disappearance on Aviles, and his reluctance to see her in the first place, I'm scared he'll hang up once I tell him who I am. Then my one chance would be gone before I even asked any questions. Plus, despite the beard, I have a feeling John Mercury won't come across like Santa Claus, especially when some kid's reminding him of something painful.

I glance at his letters, which I keep folded on my nightstand. After days of combing through Mom's papers, I found two more of them. They're dated before the first one I found, and John Mercury sounds a bit more reluctant.

DEAR ANNY,

YOU SEEM LIKE A KIND, SMART WOMAN. VERY RESPECTFUL AS WELL. BUT I CANNOT HELP YOU WITH THE NOTE YOU UNCOVERED OR YOUR COLLEAGUE'S MEMORY . . .

DEAR ANNY,

FROM WHAT YOU SAY, YOUR RESEARCH SEEMS VERY ASTUTE AND CAREFUL, BUT I AM AFRAID YOU WOULD BE DISAPPOINTED IF YOU CAME . . .

Since John Mercury's address is on the envelopes, I could write to him by regular old mail, but that idea might be worse. If he didn't respond, I'd never know whether he got my letter and decided to ignore it, or simply never got it.

I wish there was something more I could do, but I can't very well hop on a bus, train, or plane and go down there by myself. As soon as I regained my voice, I cornered my dad on the way to school since he was bopping along to a happy oldie on the radio, and even the lyrics said it was a beautiful morning. But he basically shook his head when I mentioned Aviles and kept singing off-key.

Laughter ripples down the hall from Clara's room. When Clara was about five, Neesha spent an hour combing maple syrup out of her hair. A bedtime routine of Neesha brushing Clara's hair was born. Neesha's asked me to join them, but I've always said no. It would be nice, but I feel like it's their thing. And I'd kinda be betraying Mom, since I have these fuzzy memories of her doing my hair, too.

"Homework done?" Dad sticks his head around my partially closed bedroom door.

"Yeah." I close my laptop and straighten up. "Finished before dinner."

"Good." He carefully navigates the islands of papers on the floor and makes his way to the bed. This means a chat of some sort is coming. A serious one.

"Sooo," I say, "what do you want to talk to me about?"

"Am I that predictable?" He chuckles as we nod in unison. "Fine. I've been talking with the team at the studio."

"What about?"

"The possibility of widening the show's scope."

I scramble onto my knees, leaning close. "Really?"

Dad holds up a hand so my joy doesn't get ahead of itself. "We talked about a feature story on the lighthouse keepers on Aviles Island and their community legacy. The lighthouse has been there since the start of the twentieth century."

"So what does that mean?" I don't dare ask if we're going. But we are. We have to. Please, please . . .

"This summer"—I'm holding my breath because he's drawing out the words—"when we all have a break, we'll take a drive down there."

"Like in July? When the tidings are?"

"I suppose like in July." He shrugs. "But Alice, I'm not going there to find your mom or do anything of the sort."

I jump up and tackle him with a hug. I don't care why he changed his mind, but we're going! "Oh, Dad, I love you. I promise you won't regret it."

"I'm glad you're excited," he replies, his voice muffled, "but I'm hoping that being there gives you some closure. Dr. Figg hopes so, too."

I'm squeezing him tight and bouncing up and down. Maybe he's not going there to find Mom, but I am. Closure, yes, definitely!

"What's going on?" Clara's in the doorway wearing purple pajamas, hair half brushed. Neesha is right behind her.

Possibly seasick from my enthusiasm, Dad pulls himself away and tells them about the show. Clara's looking skeptical, even kind of sour, but I don't care. I'm going to visit John Mercury, and he'll help me find Mom.

"That gives us plenty of time to plan all kinds of activities," Neesha remarks.

"Aviles Island is no resort destination," my dad reminds her.

"All the better, just us and nature," Neesha counters before Clara can rise up and resist. "Like snorkeling?"

"Cool." Clara smiles. "Think we can spend every day at the beach? Maybe get some rafts?"

"This *is* a work trip," Dad reminds her.

"We'll need buckets, too. I want to build a sandcastle fortress with a moat." To my amazement, Clara's getting on board. In fact, she's heading for my bed. Then she trips over a pile of Mom's notes and catches herself on the bedpost.

"Hey, careful," I say lightly, too ecstatic to be annoyed. Unfortunately, I don't think my tone was light enough.

"This is why I never come in here," Clara snaps. "No room for anything else."

I bend down to reorganize the papers she nudged aside. "I like it this way."

"And family meeting adjourned." Dad gets up from the bed and directs Clara toward Neesha. "It's getting late."

"Thanks, Dad," I say before he can leave, too.

"I want you to be happy." Dad turns to go, but pauses. "You do remember reading that the only way to get to Aviles is by boat, right? I have to make arrangements for us to get there from the mainland."

I nod, but I haven't thought about that part. Truthfully, whenever boats are part of any plan, I hate how my anxiety builds and builds, first starting beneath my belly button and then fluttering up to wreak havoc with my heartbeat. It's like I'm gearing up for the moment I'm not able to speak—not able to scream or yell or call for anyone if I need to. How can I get on water?

But one boat ride to Aviles will be worth it if I find out where Mom is. I'll pack plenty of paper and markers for when my voice gives out, and I'll hold on tight to Dad and Neesha just in case I want to swim back toward shore. I will be ready.

Fast-Forward

Aviles Island
July 10
The day before the tidings begin

Leo

No One but Me and Gumpa

I don't say a word.

I slip out the back door and take off.

I can still hear Baby Ansel's howling in the kitchen. I'm not sure if he's mad about cold peaches for breakfast, the twins hurling almond flour like fresh snow, my sisters fighting over the last container of strawberry yogurt, or my mom singing some old song she calls "Groove Is in the Heart" to drown everything out. Chances are, no one will notice I'm gone.

In any case, it's warp speed to the Fortress of No One but Me. My secret lair. Well, now it's mine, anyway. My grandfather and I used to hang out here together. Gumpa showed it to me. Shared it with me.

The sun's barely up. The sandy path to the beach from the lighthouse where we live is damp from high tide a couple hours ago. Dad's always saying he needs to cut the seagrass, and the long blades sting a little as they slap my ankles.

I charge straight into the ocean. I'd take the short way,

following the shoreline, but someone could see me out the kitchen window. The water's super warm, and with a roar, I crash through one wave, then another. The current pulls me easily toward the north point of the beach. My plan is to look like I'm taking a normal swim. Then I'll pop up where the rocks are. Where the Fortress is.

Mom'll kill me if she ever finds out I go there. As long as the six of us kids are fed, dressed, and relatively clean, she lets us pretty much do what we want. But she's also got a prime directive when it comes to climbing on the rocks: *If any of you children wash up on the beach with a broken skull, the rest shall face my wrath!* And she means it. If one goes down, we all go down. Luckily, we know how to swim.

I launch into a wave and ride headfirst toward the shore. The rocks are massive and made of coquina, thousands of years old. Even if you stand inside the lantern room at the top of the lighthouse and press your nose to the window, you can't see the entrance to the Fortress. It's a cave, one of too many holes to count. The rocks stretch for half a mile.

I push myself up, everything dripping. My hair's not long, not short, and feels just plain hot. Gumpa would call me a ragamuffin. If he was here, he'd take clippers to it for sure.

I climb the first set of boulders, then leap from one rock to another with solid precision so I don't slip. As I jump, something glints below me in a tide pool. I land hard, crouching to peer a bit closer. I expect to see some kind of litter and, sure enough, sticking halfway out of the water, along with a handful of shells, a few sticks, and some skinny fish trying to find their way out, is a coffee can wedged dead center in the crevice. Ugh.

I frown. I *hate* trash in tide pools.

I scramble down into the little pool and try to dislodge the can, but it's pretty stuck. I dig at the sides, push it back and forth to loosen it. Eventually it gives way. *Floop.*

The coffee can's rusty and rather beat-up, but seems sturdy. Then I see it. On the lid, in black scrawl: *For Leo Mercury.*

My heart's pounding.

Hold on.

It's a message. From Gumpa. One whole day before any of the tidings are supposed to arrive.

And Gumpa's messages are usually addressed to *The Mercurys.* My whole family. But this is to *me.*

Watery sand drizzles down my arm from the can. I should take it back to the house and tell my parents. Not only would they be surprised, but as Mercurys, lighthouse keepers, and caretakers of the tidings, they have a duty to log it in the record book, preserving its arrival in history, like every message that has arrived on the lighthouse beach for decades. There's a whole process.

But this message is addressed to *me.* Alone. Would there be any harm in opening it first, seeing what's inside, then telling them about it? We don't even begin officially celebrating the tidings until tomorrow.

I'm on the move again with the can, bounding over the boulders and finally slipping down into a hole just big enough for me to squeeze through. I head for the ridges in the back of the cave: perfect off-the-ground seating and storage.

I'm not sure what might come first: the zombie apocalypse or my twin brothers driving me to declare an emergency evacuation from the lighthouse. I share a room with them, and they're only six, with no sense of boundaries. So I've got plenty of loot stashed here in case of long-term residence, crammed into a few watertight containers and jammed on a ledge a foot above my head. Enough to last me days.

I take a pocketknife from one of the giant tubs, hoist myself up to a ledge, and start to jimmy the waxy seal around the coffee can lid. Gumpa's notes always come in coffee cans, and inside, I'll most likely find a baggie filled with several sheets of rolled-up notebook paper with thick blue ink scribbled from margin to margin. I peel back the gritty lid.

Huh. This time, no baggie inside. Instead, I find . . . a cassette tape in a clear plastic case? The kinda thing people usually used to record and play music when Gumpa was younger and my parents were just little kids. Gumpa's never sent a tape before. And, as far as I know, I don't think anyone ever has.

I take out the cassette. Gumpa labeled one side *Play*. The other is blank. The case is a bit scratched and the corners are chipped, maybe from banging against the walls of the can for who knows how long. Gumpa always played cassettes while he cooked, what he called his "Spaghetti Soundtrack." Half the songs sounded like the singers were wearing suits and dancing on air. The other half sounded like horns and pianos were fighting for space in a closet. "A lot like living with you all," he used to say.

My throat suddenly hurts, and I swallow hard. The taste of

salt water from my swim makes my tongue thick. My family returned to Aviles Island from Kansas to live with Gumpa when I was seven, right when he began to get sick. He didn't want us to move in. Thought he could handle everything himself. Most days, he could. Other days, when he couldn't, he fought my parents to prove he could. I even caught him yelling at the ocean sometimes after dinner, like the ocean was causing his whole life to crumble. One day, he brought me to the Fortress.

"Leo," he said, "your mom and dad make me feel like dying's the number one thing on my list for tomorrow, and I'm not ready just yet. But I need a second-in-command. Someone who can carry on my duties."

So I helped him with every task. On the sly. If he couldn't hammer a nail or fix a leaky faucet, I tried my best. If he couldn't bend to weed the walkways out front or climb the stairs to polish the brass in the lantern room, I'd do it. If Gumpa felt shaky on his feet, I'd ask him to hold my hand or haul (lean on) my big shovel down to the beach. If Gumpa didn't feel like eating, I'd wait until my parents were distracted by one of my brothers or sisters and slip his food onto my plate to finish for him. And on the good days, after the chores were done, we'd go off to the Fortress and play cards and eat peanut-butter-and-banana sandwiches and I'd read him some of *Treasure Island*. Now he's been gone two years, and my parents won't let me do anything I did with him. I'm back on the regular chore chart.

I run my thumb over the word *Play*. When Gumpa died, he

left me his cassette player, but no way can I play the message in the lighthouse. Even the tiniest whisper echoes through the walls. Plus, the message is for me. Me. Not anybody else. I need to smuggle the machine out here without anyone seeing. Mission on.

Alice

Maintain the Ecosystem

We're almost to Aviles Island.

We left Maryland at bedtime because Dad thought we'd sleep along the way. I'm not sure I did since I remember miles and miles and miles of blurry yellow lights and the mellow notes of Dad's favorite jazz slicing smooth through the dark. I remember letting Clara's arm spill across the imaginary line we drew down the back seat, her side vs. mine. I remember traffic shadows smudging across my notebook, across my mom's journal, and across the letters from John Mercury that I kept folding and unfolding.

Now it's morning, we're in Florida, and Dad's parking the car at the Sea Piper Municipal Marina. We get out, moaning and groaning as we stretch and move. I raise my arms above my head and gaze toward the water, which is gleaming behind a dinky pink building and two rows of boat slips. The island's out there. Six miles or so southeast. Mom must've felt so excited standing here, the promise of answers just twenty minutes away. I close my eyes and wish she could feel me here now. In search of my own answers.

"Grab your bags," Dad calls, and we drag our belongings toward the pink building where I assume we're going to meet the person who will take us across the "sound" in their boat. When we get inside, an older man in a baseball hat stands behind the register. He's chatting with a gray-haired woman in a flowered romper seated in a chair on our side. She gets up, promptly identifies us as the Joneses, identifies herself as Tina, has Dad complete some paperwork, and leads us out to the marina. Very no-nonsense.

"Why isn't there a ferry?" Clara asks Dad. "Or a bridge so we can bring the car?"

"No cars allowed on Aviles," Tina says, overhearing. "Mostly to protect the environment. Preserve the salt marsh and mangroves. Maintain the ecosystem."

My ecosystem needs a bit of maintenance as we come up to the boat. It's a motorboat and not that big, with a control panel and two seats covered by a little roof in the middle. There are two long bench seats behind, one facing backward and one forward. Tina tells Dad and Neesha where to secure the luggage when they climb on board. On cue, my stomach twists, and my throat starts to feel like it's filling with sand.

Dr. Figg tells me this feeling is "completely natural, given what happened to your mother." Natural or not, I can't let it deter me. Mental pep talk, since my real voice is probably on its way to gone.

Okay, Mom didn't really *die* in a boat. She loved them.

And she loved the water. Mom grew up sailing, even taking out a small skiff every few months or so to "make sure she wasn't rusty." Then there's the boat she took to get to Aviles Island, probably like this one. As for me, I've taken swim classes since before I can remember, so I can float or tread or freestyle if we go down. That has to count for something?

"You don't look good."

I blink at Clara's comment. I forgot she was standing next to me.

"Thanks," I say, but the word comes out sounding like a balloon squeak.

"Look, nothing's ever happened to you on a boat, right?" With two hands, Clara tightens her ponytail. "It'll be fun."

I give her a weak smile. Nothing's ever happened because I stay on land, and "fun" will be twenty long minutes.

Neesha helps me and Clara onto the boat. Once we're tucked into life jackets, Neesha and Clara decide to sit backward behind Tina, so Dad and I sit facing them. We're practically knee to knee. In no time, we're off. Though Tina tells us she "takes it easy when it comes to speed," the wind in my face and the spray from the water help me relax. I can do this.

"Dolphins!"

Clara points to a pair of fins rising and falling in a graceful arc not far from the boat. As I lean over to get a better look, the boat shifts gears and goes faster. With the slight increase in speed, I slide a bit on the slick seat and latch on to Dad's knee to keep myself from spilling across Clara's lap.

"You're not going anywhere," he says, putting his arm

around me. Tucked against his chest, I refocus on the scenery. We're still far from the island, but its green outline hugs the horizon as if it knows why I'm coming, as if it's welcoming me. Sunlight twinkles across the water, and a line from my mom's notes, something I memorized a long time ago, comes to mind. *I am called to the sea when the sun is high and turns the water to stardust.*

I repeat the words to myself like a mantra, and miraculously, for the rest of the trip, the ride's as smooth as it can be. I've even eased up on Dad's knee by the time we dock at Tina's. She has a golf cart for us to use getting around the island, and after Dad confirms directions to the cottage where we'll stay, it doesn't take us long before we're puttering off.

The town, if I can call it that, is straight out of the ancient black-and-white TV shows my dad watches sometimes. There's only one road through. According to a sign, Aviles Island is 4 square miles, population 250. We buzz past a public library, three or four shops perked up some by cheery pastel paint, and a determined-looking weather-gray cottage under a crooked but jaunty sign—SEAFOOD SHANTY CAFÉ & BAIT. People chat in front of open doors, and without the constant rumble of traffic, you can almost hear their conversations. I imagine, without so many places to be, so many things to do, they have time to really listen to one another. Time might even have a different meaning.

The road takes us past a few more buildings, then cuts through a park full of cement-and-wood benches and shaggy palms. As we follow a low stone wall along the sparkling blue ocean, the "town" gives way to thick grasses, low sandy hills, and scrubby trees. It's more wild than pretty, and the road doesn't even have lines separating one direction from the next. I feel like we're the only ones here, and we've left the real world behind.

At a bend in the road, my dad turns away from the water down a street with a few stucco cottages. When we stop at ours, mint green and the last one in the row, and begin to unload our suitcases, I suddenly notice the sticky heat. Neesha immediately goes from room to room to click on window air conditioners and closes the blinds to keep the sun out.

I share a room with Clara, which we never do at home, and claim the bed near the window. The place is definitely worn, but the wood paneling has been painted white, and the palm-tree-patterned quilt has that clean-but-someone-else's-detergent smell. For a second, as my family bustles around, I wonder how Mom made herself at home on the island. Down the hall, Dad says to Neesha that we have lunch plans at the lighthouse.

The lighthouse! Where the tidings come in and where I will meet John Mercury at last.

"The Mercurys have six kids," Dad's explaining as I hang a few shirts in the closet. "Get ready for a crowd."

I pause, not sure I heard him right. Between John Mercury's letters and the sparse info on the internet, I assumed he lived alone at the lighthouse.

"Six kids?" Neesha asks. "I imagined an old solitary

captain type in a yellow raincoat, given the letter Alice showed me and what you've mentioned to me about your experience on Aviles Island."

"Mrs. Mercury's father, John Mercury, was like that," Dad replies. "But he died a couple years ago. His daughter told me when I called to make our travel arrangements last month. She runs the lighthouse now with her husband and family, who all go by the Mercury name to keep the legacy going."

Neesha says something—and I hear my name, too—but I'm leaning against the closet door, tuning her out. John Mercury died a couple of years ago? I force myself to breathe. Nooo. He can't be dead.

I must make some awkward clucking sound because Clara snickers. "Voice coming back or chicken impression?"

Not in the mood to snarl in response, I make my way to my bed and slump on the colorful quilt. I've pictured myself sitting down with John Mercury at the lighthouse, asking if he could send a message to Mom. Then he'd help me shine that big bright lighthouse beam out over the moonlit sea to wherever she is. He can't be gone, too.

"This place is super old," Clara whines. She's trying to shake a dresser drawer open, but it sticks. She gives it a whack. The spindly beaded lamp on top wobbles dangerously, nearly toppling over Mom's journal with John Mercury's letters tucked inside.

I dive toward the book and hug it tight to my chest. "Watch what you're doing."

My voice comes out croaky, but at least it's back. Clara

scowls. "I didn't do anything. Anyway, what did you bring that for? It's vacation."

"Because it's Mom's."

"You've read it a kajillion times. Practically carry it around. Don't you know it by heart?" She eyes the journal like she's uncertain what else to say, then turns to her backpack so I can't see her face. "Thought I'd start *Harry Potter*. You were eight when you read it, and Neesha said she'd read it, too."

"You girls all right in here?" Dad asks, coming into our room. Clara says no and points to the "stupid drawer," which Dad jiggles and pulls and finally yanks so hard that he lands back on her bed, flattening a mess of stuffed animals, clothes, and art supplies.

Clara cracks up and for a minute or so they paw each other like a couple of bears, except Dad is huge enough to swallow her. She's his girl clone: wide cheeks, thick black hair, sturdy body made for things like rock climbing, biking, anything that requires moving around outdoors. When the three of us are side by side, people squint at me and say, *You must look like your mother.* But while my mom is blond like winter, my hair is more like the crayon color Tumbleweed. It also has free will—a perpetual disaster of waves and frizz.

Mom also has lots of freckles, everywhere. So do I. I have this memory of bedtimes—she'd play connect-the-dots across my cheeks and draw little maps to "special places all around the world." Then she'd make up a story. *In this little village right here, people built a stone bridge to the sky . . .*

42

I put Mom's journal down and go back to the closet. Since Clara and Dad are occupied with giggling and guffawing, I kneel over my suitcase and, as inconspicuously as possible, snag a pair of rolled-up green socks. As quickly as I can, I slip out a yellow-pink shell from the soft sock knot and wedge it in the front pocket of my shorts. Clara and Dad don't notice.

Mom told me she found the shell while on a research trip in the North Sea. To her, the shell was magic. "What kind of magic?" I asked her, and she said in a voice that seemed to skip across each syllable, "Whatever your heart can imagine. Think of the stories it could tell. Think of its journey." Ever since then, I've tucked it into a pocket or into the tiny secret compartment in my backpack when I'm at school. I haven't seen any magic yet, but maybe I will soon. Maybe here.

"You two going to be ready for lunch in about an hour?" Dad asks. "Bring a bathing suit since the Mercurys live on the beach."

I rasp an okay, tune him out, and finish hanging the rest of my clothes. For the last few months, since Dad decided we could come here, I've been trying to come up with what I might say to John Mercury. I even attempted more internet research on Aviles Island, but there isn't anything more out there. What now?

"The beach, the beach, the beach," Clara's singing as Dad heads out. "Dad said we're going to the beach!"

I'm going to the lighthouse to get some answers, from someone. With six kids, there has to be one who will help me. Voice, don't fail me now.

Leo

Get In, Get Out

I can hear what's happening inside the lighthouse before I get to the back door. The sound's like full-blast audio from an action movie. *Crash! Bang! Slam!* with lots of shouting and drumbeats in between.

I have to get to the attic.

I hid Gumpa's cassette player there, because I couldn't keep it in my room. It's pretty inconvenient if I want to listen to his soundtracks, but it's the one place Mason and Caleb don't go. Anyplace else, the twins would have sniffed it out and smashed parts across the floor in ten seconds. On purpose. Mom and Dad give them regular "talks" about respecting personal space, but the twins somehow end up thinking personal space means theirs and theirs alone.

Deciding to do a bit of reconnaissance, I slip behind the bushes that surround the house and peep through the windows.

Mom and Vivien: at the kitchen table, finishing up Vivien's

costume for her dance in the Tidings Festival tomorrow. Vivien's ten and the most like me, though she takes ballet lessons and wears things that are frilly. She doesn't say much unless she's provoked. She and Mom are talking at the top of their lungs to be heard over the happy babbling of Baby Ansel, who's in his corner bouncy seat, and Willa banging on the drums. Of course, even though she's eight, and her enthusiastic solo is sending her knotty hair and hands flying, it doesn't compare to the twins' yelling and pretend battle fire.

Mason and Caleb are on the run, Dad close behind. He's got a spaceship in his hand—and a plastic Stormtrooper mask over his ponytail. I have about fifty-two seconds before this whole scenario collapses.

I move inside, hunched-over-sprinting for the back stairs. Mom and Vivien, heads together, barely look up. Check. Willa, hair slapping her eyes, is still rockin' out. Check. Space war raging in the dining room. Check. I'm up the stairs.

The attic's tiny, its door cut into the ceiling near my parents' room. There's a rope to open it, but I'm not quite as tall as Dad so I jump for it. I graze the thing, make it swing. The drums stop.

Uh-oh.

I jump again, my thumb just missing the braided knot. I grunt, determined, getting the idea to back up and try to gain some momentum.

I take a few steps, haul myself into the air, and grab hard for the rope. The door comes down faster than I thought it would. I stumble backward, slamming into the wall. But the ladder's down, and the space war's downgraded to a rumbling assault, so I push forward and scale the rungs. Someone's feet start to pound up the stairs just as I pull up the ladder and thump the attic door closed under me.

Sweat's pouring down the sides of my face and into my hair. The attic is an airless tomb. I'm glad I'm only wearing my bathing suit.

"Leo!" Willa's voice rings out below, but moves past. She mutters about how she *knows* she saw me come upstairs.

I sit, trying to catch my breath. My teeth crunch on sand from my earlier swim. I'm dying for a drink of water. It takes my eyes a second to adjust to the dim dusty light, and when I do, I groan. My mom apparently cleaned up. And organized.

Last time I was up here, the space was a maze of odd-shaped boxes, bags, and whatnot of every size. I hid the cassette player deep inside the middle of a Christmas wreath that hadn't hung on the door in a few years. Now everything's neat. In matching containers. And labeled. But I'm sure Mom didn't put the cassette player in *Christmas*, and I don't see anything marked *Electronics* or even *Old Mechanical Stuff*. It could be any place.

I sigh and go to the closest box. When I open it, colorful fabric fluffs out. Vivien's and Willa's Halloween costumes from a couple of years ago.

"Leo!" A distinctive Willa shriek rises up through the floor. "I don't know where you are, but Mom says you need to come downstairs!"

I don't quite hear the rest of her bellowing as I open the next box (fish stuff from the time I wanted an aquarium) and the next one (some weird Styrofoam-construction-paper-paint-googly-eyed thing). One of Vivien's first school projects.

Willa keeps calling as I go through a few more containers—a tent, snowshoes, wrapping-paper rolls, a bunch of trophies with Dad's name on them—and wipe the sweat before it beads down my face. Through my frustration, I pick up on some of what Willa's saying: "Vacuum . . . bathroom . . . cheese . . ."

Those three words seem like a combination I'd rather avoid, so I continue hunting. Mom's puffy winter coat that she never wears, a set of curtains or blankets or something with elephants on them, then Dad's old Walkman thing, boxes of records, boxes of cassettes, and—

The cassette player!

I'm about to do a happy dance that oddly resembles Baby Ansel's wiggling when I hear something clanging.

Mom's ringing the bell.

Crud.

Mom rings this rusted-out cowbell for two reasons: (1) when something major has been left broken, spilled, smashed, or generally destroyed, and everybody has gone into hiding; or (2) when one of us has shirked their assigned chores and conveniently disappeared. Either way, we better report to her or the third degree begins. I have a pretty good idea that I'm the shirker this time.

I nab the player and carefully crack the attic door open. Judging by the bell and the tangle of voices, everyone's downstairs. I anchor the machine under one arm and shimmy to the bottom of the ladder as quickly as I can. In case of a twin

seek-and-destroy, I need to stash the cassette player somewhere other than my room, so I pop into the linen closet and
shove it under the badly folded towels rammed onto a shelf
above my head. Then, with my ears vibrating from the bell,
I push the attic door closed, take a deep breath, and charge
into the fray. With this amount of ringing, I may not see the
cassette player until tomorrow.

"Found him, Mom!" Willa corners me with glee before I
get to the bottom of the stairs, and the bell stops. "You have
to clean the downstairs bathroom," she tells me.

The idea makes me shudder. We have two bathrooms in
the house, and all of us kids use one. I try to clean up after
myself, knowing Gumpa would fume at the pink toothpaste
hardening on the mirror and the blue tile turning an unusual
shade of brown. In fact, on the wall right over my shoulder is
a frame with three simple rules—THE LIGHTHOUSE KEEPER'S
CODE.

Gumpa had typed them up on an actual typewriter before
we were even born. The paper is yellowed, and some of the
letters are faint, like the ribbon was wearing out. *Rule #1:
Keep the body strong, the mind sharp, and the home clean.*

The body and mind are easy, but today I'm on a different
task for Gumpa, and I'm only one boy. More important, the
bathroom is not on my chore chart this week. "Not my job,"
I say.

Willa grins. "We had a choice: vacuum, clean the downstairs bathroom, or slice the cheese for lunch. Vivien took the
cheese, I got the vacuuming, and you got the poop. People are
coming for lunch."

People? Oh, yeah, I forgot. The radio guy. Oliver Jones.

"Clean the bathroom, Leo," my dad says, squishing past us, fingers on Mason's T-shirt collar to make sure he doesn't flee. Purple marker or wet Play-Doh or some kind of alien bodily fluid covers the twins' faces. "Mom and I told you last night: the Joneses will be here soon."

Willa waggles her eyebrows and goes on her merry way. "Told you."

I plop down on the bottom step. Gumpa met Mr. Jones when his wife was lost at sea the year before we moved in. Mr. Jones came to search for weeks. "Never lost anyone in a storm," Gumpa would say on the rare times he spoke about that night. I think it hurt him too much, like a massive splinter in his gut he could never remove. "I shouldn't have let Mrs. Jones come to Aviles."

What's strange is that now Mr. Jones is coming here to do a feature story about the lighthouse and our family on his show. I wonder what Gumpa would say about that. Correction: I know what Gumpa would say about that.

Long as I'm alive, this'll never become another Fountain of Youth, like what happened in St. Augustine. Started with a sixteenth-century Spanish explorer trying to find curative waters and centuries later became a trolley stop on a cartoony map. My father came from a long line of Mercurys, and Mercurys have been the lighthouse keepers on this island for over a century. We have a community to protect. If we seed people's hope, if too many folks learn about the tidings, then the tidings, as we know them, will be history. There's a reason why we don't have hotels or high-rises on this island,

Leo. There's a reason why we're not hooked up to that world wide web or have cell phone service that's more than spotty. We won't end up a tourist trap with two-for-one attractions and cute logos on coffee mugs.

Mr. Jones coming to shine a light on the island would be a one-two punch for Gumpa, no doubt. But my mom said welcoming the Jones family was the least we could do after what they experienced long ago, and she arranged for them to stay in a vacant cottage across the island. Gumpa was her dad, and they often butted heads about how Aviles Island would eventually have to let people in and change with the times.

I get up, knowing I have very little choice but to head for the bucket of cleaning supplies. I need to make that bathroom sink shimmer, because I, Leo Mercury, oldest child, The One Everyone Can Count On, and Future Lighthouse Keeper myself, have to be responsible. And during lunch, I better find out exactly what this radio guy's up to. Gumpa would.

But first chance I get, I'm retrieving that cassette player and going back to the Fortress. I won't be able to wait one second more to hear Gumpa's voice again.

Alice

I See the Light

Since there are no tall trees between our cottage and the lighthouse, I see it well before we arrive in our golf cart. The lighthouse is a brilliant white against the blue sky. A small white house juts out at the bottom, surrounded by grassy sand dunes and sea oats bent by the breeze.

On a page in one of Mom's beat-up notebooks, she wrote that it's the lighthouse keeper's job to bring people home all in one piece, to shine a light across the waves so no one ever gets lost or forgotten. If that task was impossible, they would light the way to a safer place. I had imagined John Mercury being responsible for that, determined to watch for every wayward sailor and take on every legendary sea creature well into the night. Taking care of my mother somehow.

The man who answers the door when we knock is not at all what I expect. He's wearing flip-flops made out of rope, a faded Dallas Cowboys #22 shirt, and has a scraggly orange-gray ponytail with some weird purple streak. He sticks out his hand to my dad. "Elijah Mercury."

"Oliver Jones."

They shake.

When we step inside, a tidal wave of greetings surges toward us. Suddenly, in this tiny entry that smells like museum furniture, thrift store clothes, and pine cleaner, about ten people are shoulder to shoulder. Two sets of parents, Clara, me, five kids, hellos, and first names crashing all together. Helisaylenilivianmasebello?

I do make out the words "Baby Ansel," who is most definitely the baby in a onesie stretching over Mrs. Mercury's shoulder. Plus, Neesha's cooing at him and stretching her face in ways I've never seen.

We roll in a noisy wave toward the kitchen. The older girl of two, with a long reddish ponytail, protects a cheese plate from twin boys, probably about six, who I dub Thing 1 and Thing 2. The girl's smiling, even though the boys are jumping around her like they're dogs and she has dog treats. She seems responsible and friendly. I bet I could ask her about her grandfather and the tidings. But there's no getting a word in when we meet up at the big table, especially with voices, hands, utensils, and bowls of food crisscrossing everywhere.

"Your trip from Maryland must have taken forever."

"You must be exhausted."

"Chips? Rolls? Cantaloupe?"

Part of me wants to yell over my lemonade: "We're fine! Now can we talk about these tidings?"

I don't, but it's almost like I did because Mrs. Mercury—Eleanor—says through the din to my dad, "I'm glad you came back to Aviles Island under better circumstances. Elijah and

I are interested to hear more about your radio show. We're flattered that you want our family to be featured."

"I'm glad," my dad says. "As I said when we talked on the phone, it's typically a local program, but—"

"We're not that fascinating, are we, Mr. Jones?" This boy takes a seat out of nowhere, sandwich in hand, washed-out Flash T-shirt, smiling. Politely. The smile you use when you have an agenda, but want to make it seem like you don't. He's also got this shock of burnt-orange hair that needs weed-whacking. "What will your radio show really be about? What's your angle?"

"Angle?" My dad looks unusually apologetic, while the boy's mom and dad snap "Leo!" at the same time.

Dad raises a hand, his signal for, *Easy, it's okay.* "My show is about family and community. So my listeners might be interested in learning more about your lives and how it feels to represent generations of lighthouse keepers."

"And that's it?" Leo takes a bite of his sandwich.

"I'd like to learn more about the island," I say, sensing the perfect opportunity to turn the conversation my way. "Especially the tidings."

Leo's parents look surprised, as does Leo. Dad, on the other hand, looks mortified.

"That's not why we're here," Dad says calmly, but his quick glance toward me tells me he's anything but calm.

"How do you know about the tidings?" The color in Leo's cheeks blazes to match his hair. "They don't have anything to do with people off this island."

"They might," I counter. "You don't know."

53

"I do know," he retorts.

Dad and Mr. Mercury bark their disapproval at me and Leo simultaneously, then exchange embarrassed laughs the way parents do.

"Mr. Jones may be here to focus on us, Leo, but Alice has a point," Mrs. Mercury offers, jiggling the baby on her lap. "When people learn about other places and other ways of life, they gain new perspectives. They might even change."

"Things change enough on their own," Leo says.

As he dives back into his sandwich, the younger of his sisters, red hair in braids, pushes away from the table. Clara follows her move. "Can we go play?" the sister asks.

The Mercurys take a second to decide, which is a second too long. One twin shoves the other. The other shoves back. Milk spills, milk floods.

"Vivien, grab some paper towels," Mr. Mercury instructs, and the older sister grabs a roll from the counter, does exactly her fair share of blotting, and backs out of the kitchen with a hasty "I'll be in the dining room finishing the hem"— whatever that means.

What it means for me is that I won't be able to talk to Vivien about the tidings. I debate whether to shout, *Wait!* but she, and my after-lunch plan, dart out of the room.

With a surprisingly patient smile, Mrs. Mercury mops up the milk. Mr. Mercury's got the twins in a tight bear hug and apologizes over their heads. "Never a dull moment around here."

I glance down the table. Leo's chewing like nothing unusual is happening, even though he started the whole thing. That's when I see an opening. "Mr. and Mrs. Mercury, I would very much appreciate hearing more about your tidings tradition."

Leo's mouth stops moving. I'm pretty sure he wants to throw what's left of his sandwich at me.

In my peripheral vision, Dad's glaring at me for my timing. "Alice, stop."

"There is a lot to take in. Leo," Mrs. Mercury says, unfazed, "why don't you take Alice around the lighthouse while we finish up here? Tell her about some of the history."

Leo stares at me, then at his mom, as if weighing his options. I try to hide my dismay. Battling Leo the Discourteous for information isn't how I saw this playing out, but he probably knows as much as his sister does.

"Fine," he agrees, popping the rest of his sandwich into his mouth. He's got a lot more freckles than I do. Connecting the dots would be a mess of ink.

I follow him along the creaky wood floor into the narrow hallway. Framed black-and-white photographs of the lighthouse and the town march along the wall, dated in pencil. Mom probably loved these. She had so many history books in her collection.

Leo recites facts about the lighthouse in super-speedy tour-guide style, even gesturing on cue. He does know his stuff. Stuff about how his great-great-whosiwhatsit was the first lighthouse keeper after the lighthouse was built. Stuff about how life was back then. Stuff about sailors and how the door-frames were built from wood brought back by pirates. It's interesting, for sure, but not what I want to know.

"And how do the tidings fit in?" I ask.

He folds his arms across his chest. "You never said how you know about them. It's not something we advertise."

"They're why my mom came to Aviles Island in the first place."

"What did she know about the tidings?" he asks.

"Not much. She found a letter someone forgot in an old book, and then a colleague shared a memory with her about Aviles. She wanted to find out more." I'm trying to stay conversational, even though hostility's coming off him in waves. "Mom was an anthropologist. She wanted to study this place."

"Study this place? Like we're lab rats?"

"Not that kind of scientist." I can't help but shoot him a dark look. "She collected stories from all over the world."

"What kind of stories?"

"About how in certain places, death isn't final because people can communicate with each other across space and time."

Although Leo's skeptical expression hasn't wavered, I can tell he's thinking, considering. I decide to take advantage of the split second and gesture toward a photograph of somber faces in front of a building reduced to rubble, hoping to get back on track. "What's that?"

"A store in town. After the Great Gale."

"The Great Gale?"

"A storm unlike the island had ever seen. Back in 1949." Leo shifts uneasily, like he's debating whether to keep talking. He turns abruptly to lead me up some tight steps. He climbs a few before speaking again. "There wasn't any warning. It blew in from the ocean in the middle of the night and stayed for three days. Destroyed everything on Aviles, except this lighthouse. When the sun finally came out, those who survived found the first messages on the beach here. Notes in all kinds of containers, from the people who were washed away. The survivors called them tidings, for the unexpected good news. They showed up for three days, just like the storm itself."

I'm riveted. This is exactly what I want to know. "But how could those who died send tidings?"

Leo takes his time to reply, definitely still on guard. "Nobody really knows. Some talk about it being a divine moment, like the storm opened some sorta bridge to the 'other side.' Some say the survivors mourned so loudly that those who had drowned heard them, couldn't bear the sorrow, and found a way to send word that they were okay. And some don't want an explanation at all. They consider it a blessing."

"And tidings have appeared every July ever since?"

"Yeah, for three days."

"Does everyone on Aviles Island get a message?"

"Mm-hmm."

Uh-oh. He probably thinks he's told me too much. I'm losing him. I have to be patient, casual. I seem to have plenty of time, though. There are at least a hundred steps in this place.

I smile as we continue upward, even though he can't see behind him. Neesha insists you can hear friendliness in someone's voice, and she always gives good advice. "My dad told us that tomorrow the island's having a festival for the tidings. Is that where people get their messages?"

"No. The festival is to kick things off and celebrate the tidings coming in. My family delivers the tidings later in the afternoon."

Not extremely detailed, but it's something. "And where exactly do the tidings come in?"

He doesn't answer as we spill into this bright room, all windows and sunlight. Right in the center, there's a glimmering bigger-than-me glass sculpture, an array of prisms that could open a portal to worlds beyond this one. The lighthouse lantern. "Wow."

I move to the windows. In one of my mother's folders, she kept a photo of an ocean like this one. This shade of thundery purple, with a path of sun-stars all the way to the blinding, endless horizon. On the back, she wrote: *No end?*

Mom is out there. Alive.

I know it.

"Leo—" I've gotta ask, even though I can't bring myself to look away from the view. "How do I send a message of my own?"

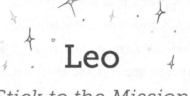

Leo

Stick to the Mission

Dumbstruck.

That's exactly the word for the way Alice Jones looks right now, practically pressing her nose against the glass. I get it. I know every inch of that ocean, every inch of that beach, but I could still watch it for hours. In fact, today there's this golden light on the water I've never seen before, stretching out over the waves.

She's also as tall as I am, and her hair makes me think of snarls of dried seagrass wrestled into a barrette. Her freckles are way darker than mine—and I've never seen anyone but my sisters splattered with so many. She doesn't look like the girls at school, who have sand in their ponytails and go around barefooted when they can. Which is probably why I didn't react immediately to what she asked me.

Anyway, the tidings are our tradition, and I can't get into that now. I have a job to do. Listening to Gumpa's whole-day-early-even-before-the-festival-starts message, addressed to *me*. And I've already lost so much time this morning.

I inch toward the stairs. "You can stay here as long as you want. The view is pretty nice from up here."

Okay, good. My foot's near the top step. But Alice looks away from the window and blinks at me, like she's a teacher and I wasn't paying attention and there's a pop quiz. Caught in my tracks.

"It's amazing," she says. "The water seems to change color every second."

"Yeah, if you go down to the beach later, you'll see the water's got flecks of gold in it."

"It does?" Alice turns back to the view. "Aviles Island is so beautiful in unexpected ways. I'm surprised more people don't come here."

"There's not much to do. No glass-bottom-boat cruises. No charter fishing tours. No motels. No souvenir shops." The mental image of a fluorescent-green T-shirt with *Good Tidings!* printed across it makes me shiver. "Of course, when your dad's radio show airs, this place could become some afterlife theme park."

She whips around to face me. "Why would you think that?"

"Come on, if your dad broadcasts the tidings tradition across the airwaves, don't you think that would happen?"

"His show will be about your family," she notes.

"Guess we'll find out." I start to go.

"Wait." She gestures toward the lantern light. "Do you actually turn that on?"

"Every night," I say. "We take turns. It's a working lighthouse."

I love that light. Gumpa never wanted to automate the lens, as he reminded us basically any time the word *technology* came up in a sentence. But the nineteenth-century parts broke down too often and for too long to be practical. Then, when Gumpa got sick, we modernized. It was easier. But he insisted on some control. Even though lighting the modernized lantern only meant flipping a switch, he made us all gather to do it. But since he died, the family ritual has become disorganized at best.

"How does it work?" Alice wanders around it admiringly.

I'm slowly moving back toward her. I need to go, but *it's the light.* "It's computerized now, but didn't used to be. It's called a Fresnel lens. It was put in just before the Great Gale."

"How far does it shine?"

"Twenty-five miles or more officially, according to my grandfather."

"And unofficially?"

Gumpa's voice rings strong and clear through my brain, and I repeat what he always told me: "*You can't measure the distance between home and someone lost.*"

"Do you really believe it can go that far?"

My stomach skitters a bit, and I feel like everything depends on my answer. "I like to think it does."

Alice's eyes widen as if what I said let her in on some secret to the universe. Even though it's unusual, and I guess pretty nice, to have someone listen to me for more than twenty seconds, I have to escape the conversation and get to Gumpa's tape.

"My mom wrote to your grandfather, you know," she says,

stopping me as I head out. "He gave her permission to come here."

That doesn't compute. I know Alice said her mom wasn't *that* kind of scientist, but Gumpa's voice tolls through my head. *Folks'll come in here and dissect our traditions like they're science experiments* . . . Whenever he said things like that, I got this picture in my head of a lab filled with our messages and memories under microscopes. So why would he let Mrs. Jones come here?

My head's swimming. I'll have to ask Alice or my parents that later. Gumpa's message first.

"I have some things I gotta do," I say, moving to the steps. "Feel free to hang out here for a while."

"Thanks." She nods, and I'm home free. When I get to a lower landing, I pause, listening. Based on laughter, scolding, and a clatter of talking, the adults are still in the kitchen with the twins. Willa and Alice's sister are in the bedroom that Willa shares with Vivien. I'm not picking up on any noises from Vivien and Baby Ansel, so she could be trying to settle him in for a nap.

I dart to the linen closet to retrieve the cassette player. All I have to do is go downstairs and out the front door, around the side yard, and toward the beach. If I'm quick, everyone will be too busy to see me dash down the beach, taking the shortcut to the Fortress.

I hunch in the hallway, listen again. The talking is louder and so is the laughter. The coast is clear, for about a minute. Ready.

"Hey, Leo, about sending a pers—"

I jump higher than when Vivien sees a mouse, not expecting Alice's voice at my shoulder. I think a pathetic, bleating yelp even flies out of my mouth because the cassette player flies out of my hands.

To my horror, the machine smashes against the wall. Big and small pieces splinter everywhere.

"Nooo . . ."

I'm moaning and on my knees, scrabbling to see what I can salvage. Alice murmurs something, but unless she's a magician and can put this thing back together with a spell, I don't care.

My eyelids burn, and I've got about ten seconds before I start crying. Then I hear my mom. She must think blood is involved. "Leo? Alice? Are you all right?"

I can't look up from the wreckage: I'm pressing buttons, jiggling the thing, popping out the batteries, putting them back in. Alice is explaining to my mom that she scared me by accident, and suddenly I'm standing up, shoving past them—and whoever else has gathered—toward the room I share with Mason and Caleb, and slamming the door. I lock it, kick a chair against it.

I sit on my bed, Gumpa's broken machine in my lap, and let the tears roar out.

Alice

Can I Help?

I apologize to Leo's parents.

Neesha apologizes to Leo's parents.

Dad apologizes to Leo's parents.

I offer to pay for what was broken.

Dad offers to pay for what was broken.

But the Mercurys say no, the cassette player was past its prime. "Please don't worry about it," Mrs. Mercury says with a smile. "Nothing in this house ever stays whole for long."

But it was 100 percent my fault.

When Leo left the lantern room, I saw my window for answers closing fast. He definitely didn't like my dad being here and didn't readily want to share any information about the tidings, but it was clear Leo knew a lot. And I couldn't just let him go without asking one more time about how to send a message.

So I chased him down and literally wrecked everything.

It also stinks because I know how he feels.

When Clara was learning to walk, she broke a glass snow globe that was a Christmas present to us from Mom. We were taking turns, making it blizzard down on this crystal kingdom where seahorses somersaulted with mermaids, and it was my turn to shake the snow. Clara wanted one last shake and I grabbed for it. The globe flew and crashed. Glass and water and magic spilled across the floor.

Clara was too young to blame, but I had shattered like Leo did when the cassette player broke. I hid in a closet for an entire afternoon. This is why Clara doesn't know about the shell Mom gave me.

There's something special about Leo's cassette player and I feel bad about it, though I don't know what to do. My dad thinks we should head back to the cottage after the fiasco, but Mr. Mercury dismisses the suggestion. "Why don't you take a walk on the beach? You can't come to the lighthouse without sticking your feet in the water."

Neesha decides to hang back with Mrs. Mercury and keep an ear out for Clara, so after putting on my bathing suit and slathering up with sunscreen, I set out with Dad.

It's the first time we've been alone since we left Maryland. I don't want to wait for him to start lecturing me about what happened with the cassette player, so I fill the silence as we walk toward the ocean. I tell him about the amazing Fresnel lens and how Leo gave me a rundown of the lighthouse's history. When we get to the waterline, it's postcard-perfect. The ocean gleams every shade of blue under the sun. The sand is blindingly white. In the distance, the beach trails off into an imposing formation of craggy rocks.

"Did you and the Mercurys talk about anything interesting while Leo and I were upstairs?" I ask, my head slightly nudging Dad's arm.

"Just got to know each other a little," he says as we kick through the rushing foam. "Some family background, old photos, that sort of thing."

"Did they tell you what happened during the Great Gale?"

"Your mom told me something about the storm before she came here," he admits, "but yes, the Mercurys did share the story."

"So what do you think now?" I jump over a small wave. "Do you believe in the tidings?"

"I believe that the tidings are a strong foundation for this island's lore," he says. "They've helped shape the lighthouse keeper's role in the community. But I'm more interested in the Mercurys and how their lives have been shaped by their family's longevity on the island. I also want to talk to more people at the festival tomorrow, to get their thoughts."

"Can I go around with you? Listen to what people say?"

I'm not giving up on Leo, even after wrecking his cassette player. But on the off chance one last sincere attempt at groveling doesn't work before we leave the lighthouse, I need to find other ways to get information. And Dad says multiple sources always give you a more complete picture of things.

Dad might not be asking about the tidings directly, but you never know what answers he might get.

"Somehow I think you'll do more than listen." Dad's grinning, though I'm pretty sure that behind his mirrored sunglasses there's hesitation.

"Isn't that what assistants do?"

Dad's smile fades a tiny bit. "As long as you remember that I'm here to find out more about the Mercury family and the island. I'm not asking questions about your mom."

"I know."

"Do you?" he asks softly. "I asked questions a long time ago, Alice. Lots of questions. About weather conditions, tides, survival rates in the ocean. And each time, I got the same answer. Your mom wasn't alive. It's not a time I want to relive. And from the bottom of my heart, I hate to see you experience that pain."

His hand bumps mine, and I take it. Our entwined fingers feel plump from the heat. "It's okay, Dad."

Sighing, Dad studies the horizon as if there's more to say in the clouds. He doesn't come up with anything. Sweat trickles down my face and into the curve of my neck.

My big toe nudges a shell, so I let go of his hand to pick it up. The shell's dull and gray on one side and, when I turn it over, a shiny, stripy purple. I rub it between my fingers. I throw the shell as hard as I can, wondering how deep it's going to sink after it hits the water. I stop to watch it go.

Shiny gold flecks dot the white sea-foam and wash across our feet like glitter. The quote from my mom's notes ripples through my mind again. This time, I recite it aloud. *"I am called to the sea when the sun is high and turns the water to stardust."*

"That's very poetic."

"Mom wrote it."

"In her notes?" He's not smiling, but there's a remembering in his face. Something that opens his eyes a little wider, lifts his mouth slightly. "We had very different styles. I was a news reporter, and she was—"

"Magic?"

My dad shakes his head with a dry laugh. "I was going to say as courageous and curious as Indiana Jones, but yes, she had a love of finding the magic in things."

Indiana Jones is a daredevil archaeologist in this 1980s movie series we got Dad for his birthday one year. "You sound like that's a bad thing."

"No, no. It's just . . ." He trails off, a wave breaking hard against his knees. "You know, Alice, from those papers in your room. She didn't mind that her curiosity took her around the globe. She wanted to find a way to preserve the future. But someone had to live in the present or everything would float away."

We stand there for a second, water sloshing around our legs, feet sinking farther into the sand. "Things were much simpler when you were younger," Dad says eventually. "You'd ask questions like, *If we swam straight out, would we fall off the world?*"

"And you'd say?"

He reaches for my hand. "*Not as long as you hold on to me.*"

I take his hand. On the count of three, we race into the ocean. Together. Laughing. My heart fills. If only I was holding Mom's hand, too.

Leo

Gone-Gone, but Not for Good

I'm standing at my bedroom window, peering through the blinds. Everyone's playing on the beach—my family and the Joneses. My parents set up a canopy tent and some chairs, along with a small table and a cooler. My brothers and sisters are building a castle with Alice's sister, and my parents and Alice's . . . mom-not-mom have Baby Ansel fenced in on a blanket between them. I don't see Alice or her dad.

I've been in this room for about an hour. I could use some water, and that sandwich I snarfed at lunch lasted all of two minutes. And since no one's really missing me, I could try to fix the cassette player.

I go down to the kitchen, broken cassette player under my arm. The only noise comes from the creaks and whirs of the window AC units and the crash of the waves. Perfect. I grab a bowl of mac and cheese from the fridge, heat it up for twenty seconds, find a fork, and I'm out to the garage.

Gumpa's tools are there, hanging neat and orderly across a

wall of pegboard. In the corner, propped up on two wooden cradle stands under a tarp, is a rowboat Gumpa and I used to work on together. The *Buoyant*.

It's not much, just plywood and a couple of planks for seats. But an old friend was giving it away, and Gumpa thought it would be perfect for our adventures, so he swapped his one-man kayak for it. He told me the boat had plenty of float left for us. Me and him.

But we never got to use it, and I haven't touched the boat since he died. I keep saying that one day I'll prove her seaworthiness again. *She doesn't need much more patchin' up to get her back out there*, Gumpa would say if he were here now. *What're you waiting for, Leo? The tide to invite you?* Gumpa had a plan, one he told me more than a few times. I just haven't wanted to take it on myself.

I polish off the mac and cheese in two massive forkfuls, set the bowl down on the worktable, and turn my attention to the cassette player. I unscrew stuff, try to glue stuff. Nothing spins, clicks, or plays. I should ask Mom for help; she's good with tools. *Your grandfather put a drill into my hand before I could talk*, she reminds us a lot. But she'd ask a lot of questions. Dad's not that curious or snoopy, but he's much better at gardening. Beyond that, fixing a cassette player wouldn't be a priority for either of them. My brothers and sisters take up every one of their waking seconds, and for the next few days, tidings duties will add more than enough to that.

I'm staring at the useless machine and the mess I've made of Gumpa's worktable when I hear the gritty scrunch of shoes on our gravel driveway. Hoping to gain more time alone, I slump to the floor, my back to the table leg. With any luck, maybe it's Dad getting the mail or the Joneses getting ready to leave. No one will even come in.

"Leo?"

It's Alice. She's squinting into the darkness of the garage, hand over her eyes. I think about not answering in hopes she'll go away. But I'm pretty sure Dad or Mom sent her here to find me, and her going back in without seeing me might cause more trouble than it's worth. I stand up. "Hello."

"Oh, hi." She blinks, obviously trying to adjust to the light. She's wearing jean shorts over a red one-piece bathing suit. "We're going to leave in a minute, and I wanted to see if there's anything I can do about your cassette player. Is it fix-able?"

I gesture toward the collection of parts behind me on the table. "Not so far."

Coming closer, she winces. "I'm so sorry. I could tell it meant a lot to you."

I can't say *It's okay*, because it's in pieces. And if she hadn't spooked me earlier, I wouldn't have smashed it. However, despite her (and her dad and her mom) asking a lot of questions about the island, she does seem genuine. Gumpa said folks being genuine is folks being generous.

"It was my grandfather's," I say simply.

Alice looks around the garage, ultimately pointing to the awkward mountain of tarp over the *Buoyant*. "What's under there?"

"My grandfather's boat. It needs some sprucing up."

"Oh." She scrapes her flip-flop in the dust on the floor, making a half-moon. "I have another question."

"What?"

"You get tidings from your grandfather, right?"

"Yeah." I wait for Part 2. Alice Jones is not going to give up.

"So if your grandfather can send you tidings, and he actually . . . *died*, is he really . . . I mean, do you think of him as really . . . *gone*-gone, for good?"

I lean against the worktable. Her question zeroes in on something I've never shared with anyone, something I can't share with anyone. Gumpa was sick for a long time. He fought for a long time. We took him to the hospital. We watched his body fade away, but his spirit hung on. Eventually, that went, too.

Some afternoons, when I sit by myself on the dark wet sand during low tide and watch the ocean crawl farther and farther toward the horizon, I try to picture where Gumpa is exactly in the big wide world, where all the people who have gone from Aviles Island are. I imagine my social studies teacher pulling down the map near the blackboard, pointing in the ocean near Bermuda or maybe Greenland or even Africa, tapping at this there-not-there place, like Atlantis or Neverland or King Arthur's Avalon. I've even combed Gumpa's old messages for clues. But I never land on an answer.

"I know Gumpa's never coming back, but he's within reach. Somewhere," I answer honestly.

"Is it like when you lose something in your house, and

can't find it, but you know it'll turn up?" Alice asks. "Like somehow, knowing it's somewhere safe in the meantime makes you feel better? That's how I feel about my mom. Only I know she's going to turn up."

"I've never heard anyone describe it that way," I say, her explanation making a lot of sense. It's just faith and trust. Like with the tidings themselves. No one on Aviles Island knows completely how they work. Even Gumpa didn't. But I believe, my parents believe, everyone on this island believes because they can recite the history of how the tidings began, and they've seen the tidings wash up year after year for generations. We've all read messages. We've all sent messages of our own back out to sea. We know because we live it.

Gumpa's words come to me. "Rule #2 of the Lighthouse Keeper's Code," I recite. "*The light of life will always burn if you believe.*"

"Something my mom would say," Alice remarks. "But what is the Lighthouse Keeper's Code?"

"A few rules my grandfather lived by."

"I wish I had met him." She perches on the edge of the stool next to the worktable. "That's why I wanted to come here, you know. I read his letters to my mom and wanted to talk with him about her. Since he was the last person she saw."

"He wasn't a softy," I say with a smile. "But he tried to teach me everything he knew. And never ran out of stories."

"Tell me one."

"Nooo." I can't recite Gumpa's stories half as well as he could.

"C'mon. You can't talk about telling stories and not tell one. You already put it out there."

Her grin's almost a dare, so I begin what Gumpa called the skin-and-bones-stowaway story, when he was seventeen and left home for the first time. With every word, I wonder if I'm doing him justice and worry that I'm messing up, but Alice laughs and gasps in all the right places.

"Alice!" Mr. Jones is calling from outside. "We're heading home now."

Alice slides off the stool and apologizes again for the cassette player. We say an awkward goodbye. "See you at the tidings festival," she says on her way out the door.

The festival reminds me of why Alice is here on the island, why her dad is here. He says he's here to focus on my family, but I can't help but worry that his story will go way beyond that, especially after the festival and with everything Alice told me about her mom. She's so keen on learning about the tidings.

I survey the sad scatter of plastic and metal on the worktable, then Gumpa's boat, hidden by the tarp. I can't forget what I have to do, too. And right now, I need more ideas or Gumpa's message will be stuck on that tape.

Tidings

Day One

Alice

What's Real?

"**M**om—I'm here! Take me with you!"

I'm jolted awake by Clara shouting in her sleep.

"Mom, I can swim! Don't go!"

I get out of bed to touch her shoulder because she's moving all around. "Clara, wake up," I whisper. She mumbles and cracks her eyes open. "You were having a nightmare about Mom."

"Wha—no—I wasn't. Leavemealone." She swats at me and rolls over to face the wall. From time to time, Clara has dreams about Mom, and I try to talk to her about them, but she never admits to having them.

Now I'm wide awake. At 3:07 a.m., according to the manatee-shaped clock ticktocking on the nightstand.

I sit on the edge of my bed, not quite sure what to do. The curtains billow in the draft of the ceiling fan. Moonlight stripes through the window. All I hear is Clara's breathing. Ever since I was little, I've hated being up when everyone else is asleep. It feels like I'm the only one left alive in the whole world. I kinda wish Clara was awake, even if she does want to sink her teeth into me. I hate to admit it, but it's times like these that I could use one of her corny jokes, like

What does a nosy pepper do?
Get jalapeño business.
Ha ha!

I reach my hand under my pillow, where I stored my mom's shell in the rolled-up socks, then tiptoe to the closet where I stashed my suitcase. I take out a notebook and a pen, and slip out of the room. The living room floor creaks on my way to the back porch, but no one seems to wake up, even when I shut the door behind me.

As I flick on the porch light and ease onto the swing, a breeze whispers through the screens. I can hear the rhythmic shush of the ocean not far away, the hum and chirp of bugs and frogs in the bushes cutting through the dark. Dr. Figg told me if I couldn't sleep to try to write my thoughts down. Maybe I should write to Mom, so I can have a message ready to go if—when—Leo finally explains to me how to send one.

So I write and write and write, until a page in my notebook looks like this:

~~Dear Mom,~~
~~How are you? What have you been up to?~~
~~Dear Mom,~~

~~Where are you? Do you float on clouds?~~
~~Dear Mom,~~
~~My swim coach says I'm getting a little better at my breast-~~
~~stroke. Wish you were here to see it. Wish you were here to~~
~~teach me.~~
~~Dear Mom,~~
~~I miss you. Do you think we could meet and catch up?~~

Nothing looks right. Nothing sounds right.
I flip to an empty page:

Dear Mom,
If you're reading this, I've found you again. Please send a
note back. Tell me where you've been.

And I cross that out, too.

It should be easy to write Mom a letter. But it has to be perfect. What if I only have one chance?

After a few more tries and a few more strikes, I set the notebook aside and pick up the rolled socks. I carefully unwrap the pale yellow-pink shell Mom gave me. *Whatever your heart can imagine.* For years, my heart has burst with imagination and stories of where Mom could be. Is it like Aviles Island, the last place she visited? Or is there another world, with normal houses and sunshine and easy rain? Where she can eat her favorite cake all day long? When you make a wish there, does it automatically come true? Is time endless?

My eyes feel heavy, and I let them drift closed. That's when I hear it, something—no, someone—talking, hushed and far away.

I open my eyes, stop breathing. I squint into the dark, as if that will help me hear. The thin, faint sound continues. Wait . . . no. Is the voice coming from the shell? Mom did say *magic*.

"Mom," I whisper, lifting the shell to my face, hoping she'll answer, "if that's you, give me a sign."

"Alice? What're you doing out here in the dark?"

I yell, not expecting a whisper back. Well, definitely not expecting Neesha, who filled the doorway to the porch.

"Oh, Alice, I didn't mean to startle you." She rushes over to hug me. Her heart pounds through her chest and against my cheek. My own heart's thumping like crazy. I'm not sure if I'm disappointed, embarrassed, or kinda glad not to be alone anymore. Pieces of all three.

Neesha smooths my hair, and I sink into the silkiness of her yellow pajama shirt. It smells like our laundry room at home. Flowery, soapy. Clara and I actually pooled our money to buy it for her birthday last year. It was a rare day when we agreed on something. Dad took us out for frozen yogurt after, because he was so happy. We were all so happy.

"Something sure has gotten into you two girls tonight," she says.

"Why?" I ask, feeling like a preschooler and not quite ready to move away.

"We heard Clara crying out in her sleep. Your dad's in with her now."

So Clara woke up again. I wonder if she went back to her dream about Mom.

When we finally pull apart, Neesha's looking at the shell, which had tumbled between us on the swing. "Did you find that on the beach today?" she asks.

"No." I pick it up. "It was my mom's."

She nods and begins pushing the floor with her foot so the swing moves gently. "You know that handkerchief I keep in my purse? My grandmother gave it to me before she died. I was named after her—my middle name, Adelaide. Everyone says I look like her." I'm starting to drift into that blurry place just before sleep. "That handkerchief's so plain, with teeny-tiny initials sewn into one corner. But to me, Granma Addy is part of me. And holding that handkerchief reminds me of her every time I look at it."

Neesha goes on to talk about her grandmother, just as she goes on rocking. I have no idea what Granma Addy looks like, but the dreamy image of Neesha as a wise-old-grandmother makes me burrow farther into her side. Finally, some moments later, Neesha whispers that it's time to go back to bed.

When we walk into the room, my dad and Clara are huddled in the dark. "You know, Clara, I understand," Dad's saying. "Sometimes it does feel like your mom wasn't real. She was a heroine in an adventure novel, always—"

"You feel like Mom wasn't real?" My voice spears the dark. With only the dim light from the hallway behind us, I can't read Dad's expression very well. In and out of the shadows, Clara's cheeks are shiny. "Mom was real," I say. "Is real."

"Alice," my dad starts, "we were just—"

"She's out there," I state. "That's real."

Neesha puts her arm around my shoulders. The warm, heavy connection gives me support, and I need her on my side. "What do you think about this, Neesha?"

"What do I think?" Her inhale is so deep it almost draws me up with it. She takes her time exhaling, as if she's checking in with every part of her body. In the end, she gives me a squeeze and leans her head against mine. "I think Aviles Island is the perfect place to figure out what's real together."

Leo
Message from Mom

My alarm wakes me before the sun. Any other time in the summer, we'd sleep in past eight. Mom and Dad would get up with Baby Ansel, and the rest of us would make breakfast—unless the twins decided my bed was the perfect place to test-drive their Matchbox cars or begin a robot take-over. But this morning, we all have a job: to collect the very first tidings. It's an honor, Gumpa insisted, to uphold that responsibility.

I'm the only one in the kitchen. I snarf down cornflakes, then rinse the bowl off in the sink. I hear a crash and thud of feet upstairs, followed by a chorus of whining and an echoing of names. No one even seems close to coming down. How can they be late when the island is counting on us to collect the tidings? After the Great Gale, the residents put it to a vote and agreed that since messages wash up on the lighthouse beach, the lighthouse keeper should be in charge. But no one is in charge around here.

I go halfway up the stairs and shout: "Time to go gather the tidings!"

Nobody answers, so I yell again.

"In a minute," Dad replies, but I'm doubtful. Even more so when Baby Ansel lets out a cry that rattles the windows.

Irritated and temporarily deaf, I move to the back door, where three red wagons and a wheelbarrow wait, complete with small picks and soft brushes inside, in case the tidings need some coaxing from the sand. I'm so tempted to start this show by myself. If Gumpa sent another message, I want to be the one to find it, even if it's addressed to the whole family. It could give me a clue about the tape. He's counting on me. And what if he wants me to do something, and time is running out?

I wait another minute, pacing a tight square in front of the door. Most of Gumpa's stories dealt with getting out of sticky situations. Gumpa totally valued teamwork. Especially when the team was 100 percent prepared.

On the other hand, if the team wasn't, Gumpa said, *Go it alone and accept 100 percent responsibility.*

No, no, I can't.

More pounding from upstairs. Gumpa would understand if I ran around the beach once to do some scouting, but Mom and Dad don't like us heading down to the beach in the dark. Sure, the sky is a light enough blue for me to argue if they get mad. A light enough blue to see sand crabs scuttling from one hole to the next. But today's too special to wreck from the start.

Mason shrieks from somewhere upstairs. I debate whether or not to go up and help, but before I can decide, there's feet-thunder down the steps. My dad's yelling, "Mush, team. Mush!"

I open the back door, just in time for the surge of bodies to go past me and outside. Mom brings up the rear and waves me ahead of her. She's wearing one of Dad's University of Kansas T-shirts and smells like lavender baby lotion.

Dad, with Baby Ansel strapped tight to his back, helps the twins haul a red wagon down to the sand, while Willa and Vivien maneuver another. I take a third, and Mom's left with the wheelbarrow.

"Checklist, kids?" Mom calls, and we all shout:

"No opening the containers!"

"No playing with the containers!"

"No swimming unless you talk to Mom or Dad first!"

"Okay, then," Mom yells, "one, two, three—go!"

So we run.

The tide's spilling into small golden pools near the shoreline. Different types of containers poke up through the wet sand. This time, I know it's not litter.

I stake out an area far from my siblings. As I scope out my territory, I recognize some families' message containers already, since they've been going back and forth for years. A round green glass with a drippy wax seal, a fat jug for olive oil, a spaghetti sauce jar with a purple lid.

No second coffee can from Gumpa.

With a small shovel and my hands, I dig and dig into the

sand. Holiday cookie tins, tight-lidded Tupperware, metal chests, even an inflatable beach ball that would seem like an impossible choice for packaging. But it's been a long-standing joke for that family as long as I've been on the island.

Not one coffee can, even from someone else.

I try harder, as if Gumpa's message is under there somewhere. Sand flies everywhere, including up my nose. I sputter and sneeze and feel like a fool.

"Quite a load already," Mom says, rolling the wheelbarrow up next to me. My wagon is practically full. Hers, too. "One of these days, we'll need to shorten the festival to make sure we have enough time for the deliveries."

"Sounds good to me."

If I wouldn't be turning my back on what remains of a tidings institution, and if Vivien wouldn't be starring in that dance routine my parents promised we'd watch, I'd come up with a way to skip it. Mom's organized a bunch of new things that I don't think Gumpa would've even considered. I'd rather stay home and keep tinkering with the cassette player.

"Not looking forward to the festival?" she asks.

"I am." I bend down to yank a plastic tub half-buried in the sand. We've had two festivals since Gumpa died, and each time, some new thing's been added. I don't think he'd like it.

"You can be honest. You don't approve?"

"Well . . ." I start, but the tub resists. Mom leans in to help. With both of us wiggling it side to side, it finally pops free. Mom nestles it in her wheelbarrow. "A ukulele band from the

Community Center? How does that relate to the history of the tidings?"

"Actually, they're playing songs from 1949, in honor of the year of the Great Gale." My mom lifts her finger in the air like she's keeping score. "And some of them are using the same instruments their parents or grandparents once played." Second finger up—two points.

"Well, what about the fancy food truck?"

"People like crepes, Leo. You might, too."

She smiles, and we continue our tidings search. I see a lid that might belong to a coffee can, and I rush over. I claw the sand away from the rim, tossing sand behind me like a puppy. But it's only a small popcorn tin. Bummed, I squeeze it into my wagon. "I think I'm ready to unload round one."

"I'll go, too."

We push across the sand toward the lighthouse, bottles and tins clinking and thumping against one another. Whoops and hoorays carry down the beach. "Hard to believe I wanted to be anywhere but here when I was a teenager," she says.

"Why?"

"Back then, the lighthouse practically boomed with silence. Just Gumpa and me." Mom grimaces when the wheelbarrow sticks in the sand, and she's got to put more of her shoulder into it. "Gumpa wanted me to go to college in Jacksonville. Since it was just across the sound and up the highway an hour, I could come home on weekends. Keep him company. Help him maintain this place. I, on the other hand, wanted to be far away from any ocean and far away from any talk of magical tides and messages."

"Are you glad we moved back to be with him?"

"In so many ways," Mom says as the wheelbarrow finally finds its groove. "This island is my family. The longer we stayed away from this place, and the more I learned about culture and religion and nature, the more I appreciated how blessed we are on Aviles to have the tidings tradition. I couldn't let it go. Somehow, our loved ones, gone from this world, can send an object from wherever they are and have it wash up on the beach. And we can send something back to them. Can we explain any of these cookie jars or bottles or plastic tubs? No. Can we hold them in our hands? Yes. We're literally keeping in touch with those we thought were gone."

The twins and Willa are squawking from down the beach, obviously arguing about something. "If we took it seriously," I mutter.

"Do *we* not?" she asks wryly. "Everything is serious when you're an adult, Leo. There are so many things to think about, worry about. Your decisions go beyond yourself. Sometimes, you make decisions that are right in the moment, but two seconds later need rethinking. Sometimes, there is no right decision. Sometimes, things just happen, and you have to deal with them."

"Gumpa didn't believe that."

"Oh yes, he did, Leo. That's why the Lighthouse Keeper's Code was so important to him. It was a simple list to return to when life got complicated. It kept him focused."

"I can't imagine life getting complicated for him."

Mom laughs as we pull up to the back door of the lighthouse with our tidings. "He wasn't *your* dad."

"Guess what! Guess what!" Willa and the twins pant from behind us. They're chugging up the small dune. Vivien and Dad with Baby Ansel are not far behind, with full wagons. "We found a can from Gumpa!"

I rush to meet them, disappointed that I didn't find it first. "Did you open it? Let me see."

"No opening containers," they chime, choosing this one moment to be good and listen to Mom.

"Everyone's here and accounted for," Dad calls. "I think we can go ahead."

We gather round Mom as she takes the can from the twins and peels off the lid, which makes a hollow *schook*. She shows us a baggie with a note inside. I hold my breath as she unfolds the paper.

"Hello, family. Everything still in tip-top shape?" she reads, and Gumpa asks what each of us is doing and what's new on the island. He sends love, tells us he thinks about us every day, and offers a corny joke about how making a boat out of stone would be a hardship. Same as last year. He didn't like wasting words.

Nothing about the tape or the message to me.

Everyone's excited and pushing to see the note, except me. I don't know if I feel let down because the message is so ordinary or even more curious as to why he sent the coffee can to me. It has to be something important. Trouble is, how do I know without playing my tape?

"Back to work, everyone," Dad says when Mom's done reading. "You can reread Gumpa's letter after we get everything unloaded and collected. One more round."

As we arrange the tidings near the back steps, Mom turns to me. "I got to thinking—Mr. Gregson at the antique store might have a cassette player. You should check it out when we go to town later."

Thistle's Thrift! "I hadn't thought of that," I reply with newfound hope. Going to town for the festival won't be so bad after all. "Thanks!"

"Glad to be of service." Mom bows with a flourish and a laugh, and I hear traces of Gumpa, the way he used to toss his head back and chuckle deeper than anyone else.

Alice

Holding the Impossible in Your Hands

Sometimes Neesha makes us watch movies from the old days like *Hello, Dolly!* when it was normal for ordinary people to break into song in the middle of the town square.

That's how the Tidings Festival begins here on Aviles Island. With the island school chorus of about ten kids singing their hearts out and raising the roof of a rustic, once-white gazebo before twirling down the sidewalk past a few craft tents and a barbecue area, past the applauding crowd.

Well, I'm not Dolly Levi, and I certainly won't be dancing through the streets, but like Dolly, I do have a plan.

Dad's recording every trilly note, and I've convinced him to let me follow him around. We leave Neesha and Clara near the podium, chatting with Mrs. Mercury and the baby, who is cradled kangaroo pouch–style. Dad stops every few people to make small talk. They're friendly, but definitely wary given that not many tourists come to Aviles. And word's gotten around that Dad's working on a story for his radio show.

But right now, he's bonding with another bearded dad in a debate over what Florida barbecue means. When they digress into how the man's using his great-grand-someone's recipe, but would love to experiment with flavors of his own, I realize this conversation is headed nowhere helpful. For me. There's just no natural opening for my big two-part question: Did any of you happen to meet my mom when she was here, and how can I send a message to her?

As my dad and the other bearded dad drone on about meat, I can't help but overhear an older couple—Visor Lady and Visor Guy—with a little fuzzy gray dog behind us. Basically, I hear this:

"It's hot."

"It's so hot."

"Even our li'l squidgy puppy is sweating."

"Li'l squidgy, are you sweating?"

I feel like saying something in a dog voice: *Woof, woof, yes, I am*, but instead I see opportunity. As Visor Lady lifts Squidgy once more to her cheek, I turn to her. "What a cute dog," I say. "By the way, I'm really curious. How do you send tidings to your family?"

Visor Lady stops abruptly in her cooing to arch one displeased eyebrow, but just as she's about to answer, Dad cuts in and introduces himself. He says he heard the lemonade stand is fantastic, and the dog would totally dig it. They laugh. He moves us away.

"Shadowing me means shadowing," Dad says when we're alone. "Not your own personal interviewing. I don't want people getting the wrong idea."

"It's the Tidings Festival, Dad," I explain. "That *is* the idea. Besides, if she'd answered my question, you might've gotten some good information."

"*Irrelevant* information." Dad points toward Neesha and Clara. "I think I'd better go it alone for a while. Think you can be good with Neesha and your sister? No grilling people?"

"Dad . . ." I plead a little more to tag along, but when his smile dissolves and he drags out my name—"Al-ice"—I reluctantly relent. I make sure he sees me stomp away.

At first, I think about prancing cheerily over to a trio of older ladies who'd probably love to help a young girl with her problem, but a silver-haired woman in a tailored yellow dress is at the podium tapping for everyone's attention. I reach Neesha and Clara the moment the woman speaks.

"Greetings, everyone. It's another beautiful day for the tidings!" she says through whoops of appreciation from the crowd. "I'm honored to have been your mayor for twelve years now, and with such experience, I know none of us are too big on speeches around here." The crowd laughs and chatters. "So let me turn the events over to Mrs. Eleanor Mercury, whose father and grandparents and great-grandparents have been proud keepers of the light since the lighthouse was built."

Mrs. Mercury takes the stage with the baby and, through the wall of backs and hips in front of me, I spy the other Mercurys standing across the crowd from us, alongside the steps. They're in a line: twins in a Dad death grip, Willa in ribboned braids, and Leo, in a slightly wrinkled but tidy white shirt, bright hair sticking out like a goat ran through it. Leo's sister Vivien isn't there.

"I'm hot," Clara whines.

I almost laugh, thinking of Visor Lady's dog, but then Clara leans into me. Her arm touches mine. It's damp and sticky.

"Ugh, gross. Can you stand over there?" I say.

Clara moves a millimeter. So I nudge her. Unfortunately, and accidentally, a bit too hard.

"Hey!" Clara staggers, bumping into Neesha.

I glance away just in time to see Mrs. Mercury take the microphone. Maybe she'll say something important. "Welcome, families, friends, neighbors. Thank you for—"

"YOW!" I yelp in pain. Pay-een. My sister. Smashed. My flip-flopped toes. With her flip-flopped foot.

I'm hopping and squeezing back tears. Thank heaven the crowd's clapping at something Mrs. Mercury said that I missed. Otherwise, I'm sure all eyes would have been on the dying tourist.

"What's your problem?" I ask Clara.

"You didn't have to shove me."

"Girls!" Neesha circles her arms behind our backs, like she's trying to corral us. Concern softens her dark eyes, but the set to her jaw means business. "What was that?"

"Alice pushed me because I was *in her space*."

"Clara *maimed* my foot." Maimed = an understatement. My toes throb.

"Should I take you both back home?"

"No," I mutter. Mrs. Mercury is still speaking, and the crowd's excitement is growing.

"Here on our island, we've had the extraordinary privilege for seventy years," Mrs. Mercury is saying, "of communicating with those who have gone from us. It's something we celebrate and honor, because we never want to take this gift for granted."

"Did you hear me, Alice?" Neesha's bending down, her smooth, round face cornering mine. The concern in her eyes has now shifted to a very limited amount of patience. "I want you and Clara to apologize to each other."

Clara protests, and my attention's split between agreeing with her, absorbing the fierce ache from my screaming toes, and straining to catch the rest of Mrs. Mercury's speech. Her voice rings around us. "Some of you knew that my father, John Mercury, had a Lighthouse Keeper's Code."

A few chuckles pop up through the crowd, along with some affectionate whistles and hollers. "I'm sorry," I offer Clara as sincerely and as swiftly as I can so we can get on with it. I want to hear every word of what Mrs. Mercury is about to say about her dad. I might learn something crucial.

"Clara?" Neesha prompts, and it takes all I have not to jiggle my hands and gesture for my sister to hurry up. She says sorry, with a relatively contrite smile. I refrain from kicking her with my bad foot.

Neesha looks at us, one to the other, dark hair frizzing around her cheeks. Her expression is ever-so-slightly frazzled, but experience tells me she's carefully weighing options.

"I think we could use some cooling off," she says, wiping her brow with the back of her hand. "If you two can stay here and watch the goings-on without further injury, I'll get some Popsicles."

"Popsicles!" Clara squeals and dives into her, arms open. "You're an awesome mom!"

Mom.

Awesome mom.

I'm not sure what to focus on, the fist-y feeling in my stomach or the flash of wistfulness across Neesha's face when she pulls away from Clara and moves in the direction of the Popsicle cart, not far away.

Sometimes I think Neesha would make an awesome mom.

And Clara's called her that before. *Mom.*

But right now, in the stifling heat, when I'm desperate to hear if Mrs. Mercury will give any more clues to lead me to Mom, when this is about the tidings, it takes every ounce of patience I have to ignore her and be cool.

I turn my attention to the stage, stopping the tingle of tears behind my eyes before it can even start. Lucky for me, Mrs. Mercury is still up onstage.

"We don't know why the Great Gale opened up a door to our loved ones all those years ago. But faith is holding the impossible in your hands, and this afternoon after the festivities, when we personally deliver what tidings we collected, you'll do just that." She jiggles Baby Ansel as the crowd claps and hoots and calls. "Until then, let's not keep our dance troupe waiting. They've been working so hard on this creative reenactment of how our tidings began."

The dance troupe is made up of kids, some my age and some a little younger. Two or three are dressed like people from the 1940s. A few others are in gray paper, some in black gauze, and one girl in ribbons of white. Vivien Mercury is in a white dress with a black-and-gold square hat. It is a mishmash of arms and legs.

"What are they doing?" I ask. Clara looks confused, too.

"It's interesting, I guess," Clara comments, "in an artistic sorta way?"

I survey the people around us, who seem to be taking in the event with some enthusiastic understanding. That's when I spot Leo and his family. And Leo's eyeballing me. Eyeballing me as if he can sense my utter confusion.

Who better to explain?

"Maybe we should ask the Mercurys what's happening," I say to Clara. "Come with me."

She agrees, and I'm glad I don't have to leave her behind. Neesha might not appreciate me ditching my sister after we've just apologized to each other, especially since Neesha could probably tell it was half-hearted.

Leo

The Price of History

Alice and her sister sidle into the space behind me. I didn't mean to give her the stink eye. But I saw her and her dad talking to people in the crowd, and he'll ultimately announce to everyone in the universe about my family and what happens on this island. It's bad enough that Alice and her family are watching this silly ballet-interpretive-dance thing about the story of the Great Gale of 1949. It's frustrating . . . and humiliating. Makes the tidings seem like a made-up folktale for a preschool play.

The second this floofy production's over, I'm going straight across the park to Thistle's Thrift to see if they have a cassette player. I need to listen to Gumpa's message to me. The suspense is killing me.

"What's this performance about?" Alice asks over my shoulder, and her sister follows with, "Is that your sister up there?"

I nod. Vivien's playing the lighthouse role. She's a good

dancer, but honestly I'm not 100 percent clear on what the leaping and gesturing is for. Every year, there's usually a skit in honor of the lighthouse keepers, not a dance. But I gotta defend it. It's our history. Gumpa might not dig the dance if he were here, but he would honor the purpose.

"They're acting out the Great Gale," I explain over my shoulder. "See? The storm's wrecking the island . . . Now the residents are being pulled out to sea. They're trying to swim toward the lighthouse, but the tide's too strong. The storm rages for three days."

"All that?" Alice looks impressed. "Wow."

"Yeah," I remark offhandedly, although if it wasn't for Vivien chatting about her rehearsals over the last weeks, I doubt I'd have a clue either.

"What's happening now?" Clara asks. Only a few dancers are left on the stage, Vivien and three other kids. One is a sun. They go through these overdramatic gestures that might represent grief.

"Less than half of the residents survive the storm," I say, then Alice chimes in. "This must be the moment when they discover the first messages on the beach?"

She glances at me for confirmation. I nod, since that would be my best guess, too.

Clara squints at the dancers in bewilderment, like she's trying to connect Alice's interpretation to the dance moves.

"Here you go, girls," Alice's mom-person says, joining us with purple Popsicles. The dance ends and applause erupts around us. "Oh, hi, Leo. Sorry I didn't get enough snacks."

"It's okay," I say as the dancers skitter offstage and a local band brings on their equipment. The crowd's shuffling and starting to break up.

"Can Clara get her face painted with me?" Willa asks, bursting toward us. Neesha and Dad both say yes, then Dad announces he's taking the twins to the bouncy house.

Perfect time to bolt for the thrift store.

I tug on Dad's sleeve and say, "I'm going around," which could mean anything from *I'm getting a pulled pork sandwich* to *I'm going to the game stalls.* He lifts his chin in what I interpret as, *Sure, go ahead,* so I move quick.

I bump shoulders with a few kids I know, saying hello as we pass, but press on through the crowd. Any other year, I'd hang out with a few of them, and we'd hit each game at least twice—football throw, Skee-Ball, water-gun blast. Losers buy the overall winner cotton candy, a slice of pizza, and a sandwich. But right now, I'm focused 100 percent on finding an old machine.

I emerge from the mass of whistling and stomping (as the band members introduce themselves) and land on the sidewalk in front of Thistle's Thrift. I've only got about four bucks in my wallet and about seventy-five cents in my front pocket. Better be enough.

I'm opening the door when a voice calls out behind me, "Leo! Wait!"

Alice jogs toward me, her hand raised in this weird low wave like she's saying hello but is simultaneously reconsidering her approach.

I wave back. "Hey."

"This is a fun festival," she says. Her cheeks are shiny from the heat. "What you were saying before, about the dance, was pretty interesting."

"That's the basic story," I say, opening the door to the shop. If the clock wasn't ticking, I'd be a little more friendly. Cool air rushes against me, along with the stale air of stuff that's yellowing, withering, and basically crying out for another chance.

Alice follows me straight back through the store, past dusty radios, boxy-looking cameras, and odd-shaped plastic telephones (a football? red lips?) toward the record and poster section. The slap of her flip-flops echoes through the empty shop. "Are you looking for something special?"

"A cassette player."

"Oh, like the one you . . . the one I . . . the one that broke?"

"Mm-hmm."

I squeeze past a bookcase, causing some old-timey *Star Wars* action figures to wobble dangerously. Alice pokes around the junk on her own, idly examining a record from a stack on a table. I scour each shelf, move autographed photos of ancient TV stars, and look under board games in rough shape.

"How about this?"

I whip around. She's dislodging whatever "this" is from between an oversize book about the Rolling Stones and a basket of headphones. The black plastic is scratched and cracked in spots, but a small orange sticker declares, *I work!* A cassette player!

"Woo-hoo!" I take the machine. Carefully. With both hands. "This is perfect. Thanks!"

Then I notice the handwritten price: $7.50.

My woo-hoo dies instantly. I'll need to talk the price down.

Without wasting a second, I take it to the cash register, Alice close behind. Mr. Gregson says hi, says he saw my mom's speech, asks how everyone else is doing these days, asks if I happen to know if he'll get a special delivery today— wink, wink.

I lift my shoulders because it could be anytime today or the next few days. I wish I knew more since Mr. Gregson's middle name is Hard Bargain, and news about a message could help my case.

I take a deep breath. "Would you take $4.75 for this?"

He's smiling, but his eyebrows quirk. He takes the machine, plugs it in, tests it. It works. "How about $6.50?"

I wince, count out what funds I have, and explain my dilemma. Mr. Gregson gives me a sympathetic look. "Six, and I'll set it aside for you. You could bring in your parents—"

"Here," Alice says. Mr. Gregson and I both look at her and see she has money in her hand. "This'll cover the rest."

I'm like a bluefish with my mouth open. *What's she doing?*

I'm about to say no, but she plows ahead. "I made you break yours. Take it."

She jabs the cash toward Mr. Gregson, and somehow I'm handing him mine, too, and in a second, he rings up the player. Before I know it, Alice and I are back on the sidewalk, where I find my voice again. I can't believe that just happened. "You didn't need to do that."

"I did."

"Why?"

"First, I made you break your other one," Alice says, swiping a bead of sweat from her upper lip, "and second, I need your help."

Even though the cassette player's waiting in the crook of my arm and Gumpa's tape is waiting back in the fortress, I'm curious. But if it's something for her dad's show, I'm out. "With what?"

Alice looks off down the block, toward the small marina where a few tired boats are bobbing in their slips. She draws in a deep breath as if she's about to dive headfirst into a pool. "I want to find my mom."

"Find your mom? Like your mom-mom? But I thought she—"

"I want to prove that she is out there somewhere, like your grandfather." She faces me again, determined. "I'm here to send a message."

Alice

So Much Possibility

Leo and I stand on the sidewalk. My heart's in my ears, and I'm perspiring a ridiculous amount. I feel like I'm running three miles in gym class, zipped up to my chin in a parka and lined tights. It's all out there. Why I'm here and what I need him to do. And I found the cassette player he wanted. Even helped him buy it. Partially. A lot happened at Thistle's Thrift. No going back now.

"The tidings are for people from Aviles," he says, shifting his weight from one foot to the other and settling the cassette player better against his body. "Not just anyone can send them or receive them. It's *our* history, *our* tradition."

"Do you know if anyone from outside Aviles has tried?" I ask. "I mean, could I toss a bottle into the ocean?"

"It isn't like fishing. You can't cast a line because you want to. Someone has to send you a message. Then you send one back in the same container."

I frown, but only for a second before an idea pops into my

head. "What if I gave you a message for my mom? To tuck into the container going back to your grandfather?"

Leo shakes his head. "That wouldn't be right."

"Please. I'm the only one in my family looking for her." I glance at the cassette player he's holding tightly against his chest. "What if you never got any messages from your grandfather? Ever. Then one day you found a way to talk with him? Say everything you didn't get to say?"

Leo pulls his T-shirt collar away from his neck with one hand as if it might help him breathe. "It's not so simple, you know. It's about being—"

"Alice!" Neesha's shouting for me.

I see her and Clara coming through the crowd toward us. "Gotta go," I blurt out, because if Clara hears me talking about writing to Mom, she's certain to make a fuss. "Think about it, okay? You understand more than anyone, right?"

"Maybe." He draws out the word—*mayybee*—as if it's filled with more anxiety than possibility. His shuffling backward is a sign, too. "Thanks for the player."

"See you soon!" I yell after him. He's gone by the time Neesha and Clara wander over. Yet I feel fluttery, mood boosted. There is possibility. So much more than before.

"Alice, I thought you said you were headed to the crafts," Neesha says.

"Oh, I'm sorry. It must've been too loud. I actually said *thrift*." I don't want to lie to her, but I did mumble unintelligibly to her on purpose when I saw Leo dart away from the crowd. I didn't know exactly where I was going, other than after him. "I saw Leo going this way and ended up helping him pay for a new cassette player."

"That's wonderful!" Neesha praises my generosity and gives me a hug. Over her shoulder, I see Clara, whose cheeks sparkle with orange whiskers and silver swirls. She's grinning through the face paint. I suddenly want sparkle and color, too.

I ask her to direct me toward the face-painting booth. Clara feigns overdramatic shock that I'm being so nice, but it's not enough to change my mind or my mood.

As we amble back into the crowd, Neesha tips her head near mine. "Thank you for the good-big-sister moment," she says, which makes me remember Mom.

When Clara was tiny, Mom told me sisters are built-in friends. Yes, there would be times when Clara and I would hate each other over toast or toys or a television show, but we would always love each other, even if it seemed impossible. Which it does. Most days. Most minutes.

When she was a baby, Clara followed me around, drooling over the pages I was reading, crawling through Mom's papers, grabbing everything I had from diaries to doughnuts. It steadily became my fault, fill in the blank:

"Alice, don't _____ your sister."
"Alice, share _____ with your sister."
"Alice, let your sister _____."

Yet today, in this second, when Clara snags my hand and says, "I can't wait for you to see the paint choices," I can't wait either. She swings our hands. Our fingers tight. Us tight.

There was this early-autumn day when Clara, Mom, and I went to a park by the shore, far from our house. Mom said Clara and I could take off our socks and wade into the water if we held her hands tight. So we ran across the beach, skipped through the cold, clear water, and wiggled our toes in the squishy sand.

"Mommy, swim with us," I begged, kicking a rainbow of droplets toward her. It didn't take long for Mom to cave, and we splashed and splashed and splashed until Clara was soaked to the frills of her pink dress, my hair was dripping, and Mom's pale blue T-shirt was sopping from neck to hem. At one point, Mom sat on a nearby rock and raised her legs, wet and bare in jean shorts, up and down mermaid-style.

"Do I belong in the ocean?" she asked, and we laughed and danced in a flurry of droplets the entire way to the car.

I've tried to remember all I can about being with Mom, and as Clara and I approach the face-painting booth, I want to ask her if she remembers that day. Yet she can't possibly. She was too young, and there's no way I can will her memories to return.

But this second, she's persuading me to have an orange butterfly painted in glitter across my face "so we'll match" (she says), and I wish the ink would last and last. That way, I could pretend Clara and I were forever this close, and she'd want to send a message to Mom, too.

Leo

Stop, Rewind, Breathe, Play

I have the new cassette player. I gotta get home.

Gumpa's message, take two.

I tell my dad that I don't feel well and want to go rest, though I don't think I look sick-flushed, just summer-flushed. I stashed a skateboard under one of the middle seats of the golf cart before we left this morning. In case someone (me) needed to make a quick exit. To the Fortress of No One but Me.

Dad studies me over Baby Ansel's head. He's sitting at a picnic table in the shade with a twin on each side, their noses deep in funnel cakes. Baby Ansel's fighting to stay awake and doing the head-bob thing. Apparently, Dad took over the baby pouch from Mom, who's huddling in intense conversation across the crowd with Alice's dad, Mayor Estrella, and a couple other people.

"So are you actually going home to get some rest or"— Dad appraises me wryly—"are you going home to be without *the rest* of us for a while?"

I scowl at his pun, but decide to choose neither option A nor B. "Can I go?"

"You honestly want to hike back across the island in this heat?"

I admit to having my skateboard. Dad lifts his brows in consideration.

"Well, that's convenient." He makes me sweat a few more seconds in silence. "You can go only if you keep to the beach road and go straight back to the lighthouse. If, somehow, you get into trouble, I will heed your call, but I'll also deny that you asked permission if your mother shakes me down for an explanation. Between helping to coordinate the festival, organizing the tidings collection, and getting them ready for deliveries, she already has a lot to think about, Leo." He tilts his chin toward the cassette player, which I'm hugging protectively. "Did you get that from the thrift shop?"

I confirm and tell him how Alice Jones chipped in. I still can't believe she did that. 'Course, she did play a big role in the first player's demise. And she wants me to help her send a message to her mom.

"That was sweet of her." Dad squints at me, his forehead wrinkling. Something more is coming. "I know Gumpa gave you the other player, so it had sentimental value. But what do you need with another one? Are tapes making a comeback?"

He sounds dubious, but looks hopeful.

"I miss him a lot," I offer honestly, "and it's been a while since I heard his old music."

Dad smiles. "Ah, the Spaghetti Soundtrack. That's good stuff. You and I should do some cooking this week."

He begins to hum a song I remember, one about sweet dreams that leave our worries behind. All of a sudden, there's a tickle in my throat, and I force myself to look at the crowd around us, to think of something else. But Alice's point keeps ringing in my ears. What if I'd never gotten the chance to hear from Gumpa ever?

I get this flash of me, two years ago, the night before the first tidings without Gumpa at the lighthouse. I asked Dad if we could sleep on the beach. I wanted to stay up all night to make sure Gumpa's message came. I had to know that he was okay, and that I could reach him.

At a nearby table, Mom's still talking with the same people. Mr. Jones doesn't seem to be saying much, just towering over everyone and listening. Collecting information.

"What do you think about Mr. Jones and his radio show?" I ask Dad.

He grins. "I have a feeling there is a point in particular you want me to make."

"He's going to tell our story to the world," I say. "Then what?"

"*The world* is a bit of an exaggeration, isn't it? Mr. Jones's show airs on a Maryland station. We won't become global celebrities any time soon."

"But if those people hear about the tidings?"

Dad tilts his head like he needs to collect his thoughts. "Over all these years, we've been tremendously blessed that so many people revere our tradition enough to respectfully keep it to themselves or to share it conscientiously. But since we live in an age when a phone can do everything from track our location in the Arctic to light up our living rooms, more people are bound to find out about the tidings sometime, Leo."

"But what happens to the island then? Everything will change."

"Slow down, Gumpa Jr. They're not paving paradise and building parking lots quite yet. There's not even a ferry to get here."

"Someday."

"Leo, this island is beloved." Dad speaks softly and gestures carefully so he doesn't jostle Ansel, who has flopped forward, eyes closed. "Everyone who lives here, everyone who comes here, develops this unusual connection to it. The quiet, the simplicity, the way we build our lives in this environment that brings together the past, present, and future. It's a sanctuary. We will keep it sacred."

I glance back over at Oliver Jones, who is now talking animatedly with the group. They're laughing. Telling him stuff. Probably important stuff that will bring more outsiders in. Dad's totally wrong. If I marched up there right now and said what I thought, who would listen to me? "I don't know, Dad."

"Think positive," Dad declares, yet I know he's filing my answer inside his brain somewhere for future reference and a more extensive discussion. "You better get going. The rest of us will be heading back in about forty-five minutes to an hour, tops, after we grab a fast lunch. I'm putting your brothers down for a solid nap if I have to sleep on top of them. They'll never last through the deliveries this afternoon if I don't."

I pat Baby Ansel's head lightly and sprint to the golf cart parked in a side lot a couple blocks down. I shimmy my skateboard from under the seat and find the small backpack Mom uses for Ansel's "emergency change of clothes." Out go the clothes into the back seat of the cart, in goes the cassette player. Straps over my shoulders, and I'm off.

The air's thick and hot as I cruise down the sidewalk. The road's lined with sun-bleached cottages and wilting flower beds that also look like they're on their way to heatstroke. Since I was five, I've been inside nearly every house on this block for a birthday party, a game night, or an after-school snack. The two-story house with the green paint and manatee mailbox. The tiny place partially hidden by sago palms. The long yellow ranch house, lawn half sand, half sea grape run wild. Hang a right and there's a bright pink cottage with a yellow roof and a red picket fence. The twins' old preschool. Willa's old preschool. Viv's. Mine. It will be Ansel's, too, someday.

I want to believe Dad. I mean, there isn't a soul on this island who doesn't know every inch of it, who doesn't have a special story about growing up here or moving here. They may complain sometimes about having to go to the mainland for certain supplies or entertainment, but there's also a silent promise in the air, kind of like we belong to a secret club.

I push off the sidewalk to gain momentum. With the rush comes Gumpa's voice. *It's about those strangers who will come with impossible hope and will be devastated when they don't find any. Those strangers who will demand answers as to why the tidings come and where they're really coming from. Those strangers who will stop at nothing to prove we are fakers or that we can make miracles. Then one of two things'll happen: (1) They'll get sad because the miracles aren't showing up and we don't have answers; or (2) they'll get mad, make up answers, and turn the miracles into profit. Something's gotta give eventually.*

Gumpa prattled on (he loved the word *prattled*) about most things, from the quality of plywood to the crunch of his cornflakes. And the subject of the island could get him going for hours, with breaks in between for a glass of milk and a handful of boiled peanuts. And, in a matter of minutes, I'm hoping that I get to hear his voice again.

I shift to hyperspeed down the lighthouse road, but ditch the board in favor of foot power when I hit the sand-and-gravel driveway. Then I'm a blur—running upstairs, yanking on my bathing suit in case the cave is wet, making sure I have Gumpa's tape, grabbing batteries for the "new" cassette player, tossing everything into my own backpack, then racing down to the beach, full throttle toward the rocks. Luckily, the tide is going out when I get into the Fortress. No puddles.

Breathing hard, I settle on a ledge, Gumpa's coffee can next to my knee. My hands shake a little as I put his tape into the player and press PLAY. The machine whirs, the tape crackles a bit. It's starting.

Leo?

His voice is slightly distorted, slower than any drawl, but I'm shouting at the machine as if it's him, as if he can hear me. "Gumpa!"

The tape whines a little as if it's stretching. I peer through the plastic cover, but everything's spinning normally. The weird sound is coming from the recording. I hit STOP, rewind to the start, and play it again.

Leo?

Then it's like he's playing on walkie-talkies with me and Willa. Every word pops with static. I can barely make anything out. I lean closer to the player and thumb the volume to the highest setting. His words fall away into noise that sounds like high tide meets vacuum cleaner.

"No, no, no!" I want to shake the machine, throw it across the cave, curse my grandfather for even sending the stupid tape in the first place. Maybe salt water seeped into the can; maybe it was all the rattling around in the waves. Whatever happened, the tape's all garbled. But I have to hear his voice clearly. I just have to.

"Take a breath," my mom says when I'm about ready to clobber the twins, so I breathe and rewind the tape carefully, determined to figure out what I've missed or, more important, hoping the fuzzy first try was a glitch and that Gumpa's voice will come out loud and clear now.

Plus, I cannot in any way afford to break this cassette player.

Before pressing PLAY again, I grab a small notebook from my supply stash. Then I close my eyes. *Please work, please work, please work.*

When I begin again, I zero in on every somewhat-clear word. *Leo? [sshhhhkkkk] by some miracle [whsshhh] this old tape [kthtktht] I'm afraid [whrrrr] I must try [shhhhh] need your help [zhhhhk] Jones family [kllllk] trust you [zzhhhkkk] believed so much [whshhh] I want her family to find [shhkkk] the ocean will show you [zhhhkkk]*

I stare at my scribbles and exhale hard, realizing I've been holding my breath. What does this mean? And did he say *Jones family*? As in Alice Jones?

I rewind again. This time, I play it slow and stop for every word I can hear. Every word sounds exactly the same as before.

"Quiet!" I yell at the ocean bashing the rocks outside. I rewind and play, rewind and play. Same.

My brain's racing as I skim over my notes. This is way bigger than the ordinary messages Gumpa's sent over the past two Julys. What does it mean? Why did he record it just for me? Is he in trouble? He said he's afraid and needs my help. *My help.* With the Jones family. He wants them to find something. Should I tell Mom and Dad? How will the ocean show me anything?

And what about Alice? Could this be related to finding her mom?

I lean my head back against the cold rock and take a few deep breaths so I don't hyperventilate. I'll figure this out.

There's a B side. Maybe it will explain everything. Maybe it will give me all the answers.

I flip the tape. PLAY.

A second of static. Then a woman's voice says cheerfully:

Anny Jones, interviewing John Mercury [shkrrrhsh] Aviles [tk-tk-tk-tk] . . .

"What?" I say, and jab the STOP button. My own voice echoes back to me, at peak pitch and freaked out. An interview? With Gumpa? By Anny *Jones* . . . Alice's mom? Is this what Alice was talking about?

I rewind the message and play it again, this time letting the friendly voice go past what I heard. Through an avalanche of static, the woman announces the date: April 10, six years ago.

The day Alice's mom went out on the boat?

Are you sure [ssshhhhh] I could just email you [phhh-httttkkk] a copy [klk-klk-klk] John. My phone will record [zzzzhhhhh] I promise.

More static. I press my ear against the player. Gumpa now. All gristly and matter-of-fact. *I don't do inter—[chchchch] no compu—[kkkkkk] I'll have my own [ftkftkftkftk] safe-keeping.*

STOP.

REWIND.

Breathe.

PLAY.

And there they are again. Alice's mom and Gumpa. Together.

When Anny Jones came here.

I stop the tape again, my insides all churned up. I want to play it to the end, but I feel like I'm trespassing. Alice needs to be a part of this. Even though this is just some scratchy old recording, these may be her mom's last words.

What if Alice's mom and Gumpa are both in trouble?

Alice

What Do I Want to Know?

Clara and I are telling goofy jokes about butterflies, balloons, and tuna fish as we walk with Neesha back to the golf cart where Dad's waiting. I'm also half thinking about Leo and when I might see him again to convince him to help me send Mom a message.

When we get to the golf cart, Dad has this look.

The look.

I try, try, try not to let my butterfly mood flutter away, but the look makes my stomach hurt. Because it's only appeared once before. When Dad got the phone call about Mom. How could I ever forget that moment?

What's wrong, Daddy? I asked then.

When I was six, my dad was take-on-the-world strong. Giant and solid. But he didn't answer me.

I could hear the voice on the other end of the phone. Whoever it was had found the sailboat Mom had rented for the afternoon. But they hadn't found her, or any signs of her. Then came the look in Daddy's dark eyes. It changed with each slow blink. Like he was fighting hard not to believe what they were saying, but had to.

Now, as we settle in the golf cart, Neesha asks Dad if he's okay, and he says yeah, but she drives us home, him beside her. She knows something's up. Even Clara asks.

"I'm fine," Dad answers firmly, which tells me he totally isn't, and stops me from chiming in.

When we stumble into the cottage and dump our grubby selves onto the couch, grateful for the air-conditioning, Dad still has the look. When Neesha asks how his morning went and what he learned about Aviles Island, Dad still has the look.

He begins a sentence, then stops. Begins another sentence, then stops. With an unsure laugh that fades away. The sound doesn't make my stomach feel any better, but I can only think of one reason for the look. The faltering. I was there. I remember.

"Did you find out something about Mom?"

I can't help myself, I have to ask, even though it's the same question that caused the look the first time. Out of the corner of my eye, I see Clara unroll herself from the couch and slip out of the room. She's muttering something under her breath about how "the day couldn't last forever," but I don't care. I'm waiting for Dad.

"No." His tone is tired.

"Then what is it?" I press.

For a few seconds, the flamingo clock above our heads fills the silence.

Ticktock, ticktock.

Dad takes a deep breath. "Usually the stories I do are pretty straightforward. Colorful profiles, with interview clips and an interesting hook. But no matter which way I look at it, I can't do a simple family feature about the Mercurys and their lighthouse. They're inextricably bound to the tidings, as is everyone else here on this island." His expression fills with awe. "Several people did open up to me, and their impressions and stories about the Mercurys always went back to the tidings."

"Won't that make for a richer story?" Neesha asks.

"It makes for a pretty wild one, one I didn't intend to tell," Dad admits slowly. "Either the tidings tradition is the most elaborate and well-executed sham in history, or the residents of Aviles Island can actually talk to dead people. Both possibilities blow my mind. Feels like an episode of *The Twilight Zone*."

I get it now. That old black-and-white TV show is chock-full of strange happenings that turn belief and disbelief inside out. Dad can handle fact, but can't deal with a premise that leaves him with spiraling questions and uncertainty that he has to accept as the truth. I sit up straighter on the couch, wanting to hear what else he has to say.

"You've tackled some incredible features before." Neesha's voice is cheerful but strained. "What's so different this time?"

"The entire town, from mayor to toddler, has such conviction."

"Like Mom did," I remark. Maybe Dad's finally seeing the truth.

Ticktock. Ticktock.

He doesn't respond, just rubs his temples.

"Are you done talking?" Clara plops down onto an armchair across from the couch. She's washed her face paint completely off, so her nose and mouth are clean, but they're scrunched with frustration.

"Yes," Dad says.

"No," I say. We're finally getting somewhere.

"You know, I noticed a theater in town." Neesha reaches up to unsnap the barrette holding up her bun. Her hair takes its time fluttering down around her face. "There are a couple good classic movies playing this afternoon. Anyone want to spend some time in dark air-conditioning munching on popcorn?"

Between my stomach being twisty and my cheeks sticky with face paint and sweat, I'm ready for some time in controlled cool.

So I nod in agreement. "What do you think, Dad?"

"I'd like to," he says, "but in an hour or so, I'm going to the Mercurys to observe their tidings deliveries. They suggested I come."

Deliveries?

Immediate no to the dark, cool movies for me. Deliveries with the Mercurys means I can talk to Leo again. I have to go with Dad.

"Can't you talk to them after?" Clara asks.

"The Mercurys are pretty busy with everything going on with the tidings and with their household," Dad explains. "I have to catch them when I can. And it's another peek inside the community."

"Count me in," I say.

I should have anticipated Dad's warning: "If you come with me, Alice, no interviewing on your own."

"I get it." I widen my eyes in what I hope resembles some model dutiful, irresistible kid face. "You won't even know I'm there. Promise."

"You and I can go to the movies, can't we, Neesha?" Clara's question is as defiant as it is hopeful. "You don't care about all this island stuff, right?"

"It's a mystery for sure," Neesha answers evenly, like she's trying to balance the universe on her shoulders and not lose focus. "But yes, you and I can go while Alice and your dad can do their thing. We can catch up at dinner." Then Neesha stands, tells us she's going to clean up and take a quick shower. Before she turns to go, she pauses in thought. "It's so hard to believe there are actual messages to deliver. From people who've been gone for years."

"It really is," Dad agrees, and closes his eyes.

Clara glares at me, as if the festival, the jokes, the cease-fire between us, never happened. The thought hurts. *You ruin everything*, she mouths.

Pretending to ignore her, I scramble off the couch, beelining to our room. I have more important things to do.

I shut the door and find my tiny notebook where I crossed out those not-right letters to Mom. I have to write a message in case I get the chance to send one. And I need to write it before Dad tells me it's time to leave.

I settle back against the headboard of my bed, legs up, frilly pillows behind my neck. Okay, one, two, three, go.

That's as far as I get.

There are twenty-five blue lines on a notebook page. And lots of white space. Expecting me to fill it. How did Mom write the way she did?

I growl at my pen as if it controls my language ability. *Think, Alice.*

Last year in English class, Ms. Rasmussen would always tell us to brainstorm before we started writing. And sometimes, she said, a list of questions was a good place to start. She'd ask, *What are the most important things you want to discover?* She'd also say, *Begin small, and let it roll down the hill.*

I glance at Mom's journal on the nightstand. Even without opening it, I can see her fine, curled comments across the pages. What do I want to know?

If you're not really dead, where are you?

Where have you been all this time?

Now that I've found you again, will I be able to write to you every year?

Can I write to you from home?

Do you have a home?

You're not dead, in the forever sense, right?

Right?

I cross out everything, toss the notebook aside, and roll over into a tight ball, burying my head in the pillow. I'm smearing face paint across the pillowcase, but I don't care.

The bedroom door opens and in walks Clara. "I'm getting

ready for the movie," she announces, like she wants me to leave or care. I don't do either one.

She tries again, this time from between our beds. I can't see her face, but I know she's staring down at me. "Shouldn't you be getting ready to go with Dad?"

"Not for a while," I mumble.

"What were you writing?" Clara snatches my notebook from the bedspread.

I hear the pages ruffle. In a second, I'm leaping after them. She's already reading.

"Gimme that." I nearly knock her over, but she holds her own.

Clara stretches the notebook out wide, beyond her body. "Is this some kind of letter to . . . to . . . ?"

"Give—me—that," I roar, and suddenly she's tossing the notebook back to me like it's a hot pan and she's not wearing an oven mitt. I gather it up and press it to my chest.

Clara stares at me. Her shoulders heave slightly from the scuffle, but suddenly she looks more remorseful than I've ever seen her. "Alice," she says quietly, and not like herself, "I wish I knew what made her so special."

Her admission sucks the air out of the room. She's never said anything like that about Mom. Like she feels left out. Does she really feel that way?

"I wish a lot of things, too," I mumble back.

Without a reply, Clara opens the top drawer of the dresser, takes out a T-shirt, and leaves. She always has a reply. Not this time. She's almost . . . sad.

She's gone before I can tell for sure. I should go after her, try to talk to her, but I know it would end badly, like usual.

I bury my face in the pillow again, wanting it as dark and cocoon-like as possible so I can't see anything. I should be ready to go with Dad, but I'm not. Why can't I write a simple letter to my mom? Why is this so hard?

I roll over. Something sharp digs into my hip, and I remember the shell Mom gave me, tucked in my pocket. When I take it out, it looks small in my hand. Ordinary. Not magical at all.

Leo

Master of the Sea

The garage is dark and hot, the kind of hot that sticks in your lungs and makes you wonder how long you'll be able to breathe. No one's gonna bug me here, not with the post-festival wind-down taking place inside the house. Dad's upstairs taking a nap with Baby Ansel and the sugared-out twins. Mom's crammed in her tiny office, organizing the tidings paperwork before the mid-afternoon delivery. And after arguing over a bracelet, which involved braid yanking and a few threats, Vivien and Willa are reading in separate corners of their room.

I prop the garage doors wide open with two bricks, hoping the sea breeze will swoop through. I would've stayed in the Fortress, but the tide's coming in. I also only have about an hour and a half before my family's circus starts again and we get ready to make the deliveries around town. Dad called Mr. Jones to invite him to tag along, which to me seemed unnecessary, but it did give me the chance to ask if Alice could come, too. Dad gave me a curious smirk, but I'm hoping she and I can steal away and play the tape. But what am I gonna tell her? *Hey Alice, wanna know something bizarre? My grandfather sent me this cassette that has an interview on it. From a long time ago. Your mom and Gumpa.*

As my eyes adjust to the shadows of the garage, the *Buoyant* looms in the corner under its tarp, like a dusty relic covered up for the ages. I flick the light switch near the worktable, though the glow from the cool white bulb doesn't go very far. Then I go to the boat and peel away the tarp.

Dust powders up into the dim light, making me cough. The rowboat smells pungent, like aging wood and seaweed that has baked in the sun for days. I was the one who covered it up in the first place. The day we celebrated Gumpa's time with us on Aviles. The day lots of people from the island came in their boats, and we sang shanties and threw Gumpa's ashes out to sea. I closed my eyes during that part. Until that second, I held out hope he would finish fixing up the *Buoyant* with me.

I swallow. The back of my throat's tightening like I'm about to blubber. Blinking fast, I head for Gumpa's worktable for some old rags and some sandpaper. I can't let his boat waste away in the dark.

I'm crouched on the ground near the hull, batting away cobwebs, when the door to the lighthouse screaks open and bangs shut, followed by someone crunching across the gravel outside the garage. It isn't Willa or the twins. Too slow. Not Dad or Vivien. Too purposeful. Has to be Mom.

"Leo?" Mom calls as she strides into the dark with a pencil jammed into the end of her long braid and a red sun hat dangling from a cord around her neck.

I stand up, shaking out a crick in my legs.

"I was going to see if you would help me bring the tidings around front," she says. Earlier this morning, we spread the huge load of containers in the sparse grass along the back of our house. After we hosed the salt and sand off, they needed some time to dry in the sun. Mom gestures toward the boat. "But it looks like you already have a project. Dad told me you got a new tape player at Thistle's, too. Tidings week always brings up good memories."

She wanders over to me and surveys the boat. "She's looking pretty sound."

"How do you know?" I ask.

"How short is your memory?" Mom gently nudges me with her shoulder. A few months and I bet I'll almost be as tall as her. "I grew up here, remember? I had a skiff or two of my own."

I grin. Gumpa did tell me a few tales about younger Mom. "Pirate Eleanor."

"That's Buccaneer Norie to you." She puts on her hat, angles it over one eye, and takes a swashbuckling stance, arm out sword-style. "Commander of the high seas."

I counter her, dirty rag pointed, and we jab and thrust and parry around the garage. We kick up sand and dust and laugh so hard we double over and hold our stomachs.

"I surrender." Mom wheezes through one last chuckle. "I've got a job to do."

Once I catch my breath, I offer to help, and once I've put away the rags and sandpaper, we make our way through the sand around the lighthouse. The wind has picked up from this morning, and the puffy clouds from earlier are racing across the blue sky.

"The forecast didn't say anything about rain for a day or so," Mom says, "but something's definitely starting to brew."

She holds up a finger like Gumpa used to, as if it has the power to detect a change in the air. More often than not, his predictions were right. I wonder if Gumpa felt the storm coming on the day of Mrs. Jones's boat accident.

"What do you know about Gumpa and that boat wreck a long time ago? The one with Mrs. Jones?"

"It was about a year before we moved down here to be with him." She bends down to shake a pebble from her sandal. "He called me the night it happened. It was the only time I ever heard your grandfather cry."

"He cried?"

"I know. Master of the sea with salt water in his veins, right?"

I manage a half smile. Even the twins know that running joke. "But why?"

"Gumpa blamed himself. He told me he met Mrs. Jones that morning to talk about her research, but he wasn't as forthcoming with his information as he should've been. He was getting sicker then, wasn't sleeping well. Guess he got a little snippy and began reconsidering what he thought she should know. So I guess Mrs. Jones rented a boat from someone for a quick sail, hoping to find answers of her own. She didn't return before the weather changed. When he found out, he and some of his buddies tried to look for her, but the storm came in too fast. The light from the lighthouse wasn't enough to lead her in."

"But none of that was his fault."

"He sure thought it was." Mom wraps her arms around her body, goose bumps rolling like waves across her skin. Her hat shadows her face. "If he hadn't said she could come to the island, or if he'd given her the answers she was looking for, he believed the accident wouldn't have happened. He felt like he led her on, raised too much expectation."

The clouds cover the sun as we reach the back of the house. I'm suddenly cold, too, but I let the shivers ripple through me. It's better than focusing on the tension pulling at my throat. Mom stops in front of the wagons we use for transporting the tidings.

"Alice told me that her mom wrote Gumpa letters before she came. Are they around here somewhere?" I ask.

"Most likely. There are boxes of Gumpa's correspondence in the office," she says thoughtfully as we start to load the various bottles, jars, and jugs into the wagons. "Perhaps the Joneses would want them. I was surprised when Mr. Jones called a few months ago and wanted to do a story on our family, especially after what happened to his wife. But closure takes its own time. The letters might be a lovely thing for them to have."

I'm tempted to tell her about Gumpa's message and the

interview with Mrs. Jones, but I don't want it to accidentally become part of Family Discussion at the dinner table tonight. Mom's got so much on her mind that it might slip. Then *To Leo, From Gumpa*, written solely for me, would be sibling fodder. I'd never have it to myself again.

"I think we have more than usual here." Mom's voice cracks slightly as she studies the wagons, now overflowing with containers. Her hat has fallen to the back of her neck, and her cheeks are slightly red. She wipes the corner of one eye with the loose waist of her dress. "Goodness, you would think after all these years the sight of these messages wouldn't affect me so much. But each one is filled with love, you know?"

I lean against her, the closest to mushy I can be without unleashing tears of my own. I try not to think about what the tidings really mean, because losing Gumpa was so hard, but deep down knowing that Mom and Dad and the people I love will always be as close as the tidings makes me feel better. "I'm glad we're part of this island."

"Me too." Mom snuggles her face into my hair, and I pull away with a scowl that I know and she knows is totally fake.

Alice

Making Peace Is Not like Making Your Bed

The sun is blistering when Dad and I take the golf cart over to the Mercurys' for the deliveries. Our little roof gives some shade, but the light is slanting through the palm trees and hitting our shoulders. I feel burnt and raw. I'm glad Dad's talking. Listening to him is so much easier than thinking about what I couldn't write to Mom.

"I can't get over this place," Dad remarks as we bump down the brick-paved main street. The ride makes his voice jittery and more lighthearted.

"Without cars, it could be sixty years ago," he continues, pointing toward a brick building, one side a faded advertisement for ELIXIR, the red paint barely proclaiming, MENTAL SUNSHINE! "People on Aviles do business with a handshake and a bit of advice. They keep everything. Maintain everything. Reminds me of my grandparents. They always made things last. Why throw perfectly good things away when you can fix them? In fact, I can remember this drawer they kept full of neatly folded recycled baggies. My nana would wash them out, dry them, and reuse them."

"Like lunch baggies? Ew." I'm temporarily moved out of my mood to comment. Having PB&J in the same baggie where tuna or turkey once lived, rinsed out or not, is definitely gross.

"Well, maybe the baggie example isn't the greatest." Dad laughs. "But they really do extend the shelf life of things around here. Like it's their duty. Responsibility."

I murmur agreement as we pass the grocery store. HENRY WINKS scrolls across the front sign in curly red letters, like the writing on a soda bottle when Nana was a kid. No, Aviles Island is not a hot spot paradise for tourists, but it's sort of reassuring the way things haven't changed. Not like home in the suburbs, where you can't keep track of all the new shops and neighborhoods and restaurants cramming every corner. Where we have so much going on, we stop paying attention. Here, riding around slowly in a borrowed golf cart, we can see so much up close. And as we drive out of the town, nothing comes between us and fresh air, tiny pink wildflowers, and the ocean. When I catch a glimpse of the water just right, it sparkles like solid happiness. Where magic lives.

Might live.

Might not live.

The golf cart bumps over a small stick, and I jostle against Dad's arm. A question tumbles out of me before I can stop it. "If you wrote a message to Mom, what would you say?"

"That's a tough one." Dad gives me an awkward, even

pained smile. "From the details people here have shared with me, their messages are so normal, like an ongoing conversation. Like no one is really gone from their world. But your mother . . . she's been gone from our world a long time now. I guess I'd try to catch her up on everything you girls have been doing, how you've grown. What she's missed." His expression becomes a little reluctant, cautious. "After all this time, I'm sure you know exactly what you'll say, huh? In your message?"

Dad's looking sideways at me with his mouth kinda crooked, like he's wondering whether he should've asked the question. Whether he wants to hear my answer. I can't tell him that I'm at a total loss about what to write to Mom.

"There's a lot to say, Dad," I answer finally, and hope to leave it there.

"Yeah, I understand that," he replies after a longish pause and a vague, distant gaze that definitely says, *Be back in a second, lost in a memory*—which I'm fairly sure involves Mom.

He must have so many memories of her. So many that he's never shared with me or Clara. He did tell me the story of how they met, a couple years before I was born, when he was a young reporter and she was a grad student at the University of Maryland, almost finished with her PhD.

She was speaking at a literary festival, in front of the undergraduate library, this girl with hair brilliant as snow and a voice that danced across vowels. He made his way to the front, not hard in the small crowd, right at the second when Mom said, "Stories don't end. They cross the boundaries of time and space. We tell stories to find our way home." In that moment, she made him wonder what happily ever after with her would look like.

"Why did you stop searching for her, Dad?" I ask now. "What made you give up?"

Dad takes my left hand with his free one. He's blinking fast. A few tears catch on his eyelashes. "You and Clara needed my complete attention. You both needed to know you had one parent who was there for you."

"So you just let Mom go?" I want to say it carefully and evenly, but I kinda choke instead. "Stopped loving her?"

Dad squeezes my hand, as tight and firm as any reality check. "I had to figure out a way to love her differently."

"*Differently.*" Out loud, the word sounds misshapen, like something awkward swept into a corner.

"I carried around your mom's death for so very long, Ali," he goes on sadly, which makes my heart crack wide open. "And so have you. All I want is for this trip to help you finally make peace with it."

Make peace. Like making your bed. Smooth the sheets over the lumps of missing her. The lump of Mom's existence.

I'm this close to blubbering like a baby. I'm swallowing, swallowing, swallowing. All these years, he's tried to tell me: move on like he moved on.

He's argued with me and humored me and taken me to doctors and even took me on this trip. Beneath that, I see what I've wanted: the tiniest pinprick of hope. The tiniest pinprick of hope that he still *felt something* and that coming to Aviles Island would finally show him that Mom was still out there.

But it's suddenly and agonizingly clear that no matter what incredible insight he has on this island or about this island, no matter what he stops believing or starts believing—it won't be, can't be, about Mom coming back to us somehow.

And if he doesn't feel her love somewhere alive in the world, in the deepest part of him, how can I?

We turn onto the long gravel driveway to the lighthouse. I want to jump out of the cart and run as fast as I can off this island. So fast I'm a speed blur. So fast I turn back time and I'm in Maryland and my mother is giving me the shell that hasn't done anything magical, and this time I get to say, *No, I won't let you go. You are not going to disappear. You are not going to leave us now.*

Dad hasn't let go of my hand, and now it's numb. We're approaching the lighthouse. Behind this frenzy of Mercurys zigzagging across the front yard, there are several wagons and plastic crates filled with glass bottles, a plastic tub, a jug, a beach ball. All with notes inside waiting to be delivered, waiting to be read, waiting to be answered and sent back.

Mine won't be there.

I should've gone to the movies.

Leo

There's Something You Should Know

Alice doesn't get out of the golf cart right away when she and her dad pull up in front of the lighthouse. I don't blame her. It's all-out war around here.

Right after Mom and I called through the house for everyone to gather in the front yard for the deliveries, the twins flew outside, rustled up some water balloons, and filled them with the hose. Willa and I got ambushed the second we stepped through the front door, so we dove for trash can–lid shields, but Vivien and Dad were caught in the cross fire and are now double-teaming Mason for his ammo. Caleb and Willa are in the middle of a showdown. She stole his balloons.

Mr. Jones heads over to the safe zone toward Mom (who has Baby Ansel strapped on), probably to talk logistics. I duck behind the garage door and eye Alice, who's still sitting in the golf cart, watching the Battle of the Balloons unfold. It'll take a few minutes for the skirmish to settle down, even after Mom yells for everyone's attention. Then it will be quiet enough for Alice and me to talk.

I can't wait that long.

Keeping myself low to the ground, I dash over and leap into the seat behind her. I'm damp and out of breath. "Hi."

"Hi," Alice echoes with a soft, surprised laugh. She shakes her head quickly, like I knocked her loose from some heavy thought and zapped her back to reality. Her purply-brown eyes are rimmed with pink, the swollen kind of pink from tears that are being restrained and plan to leak out at any second.

That's not good.

I don't even like my own crying, let alone other people's. When it's my sisters, I apologize if their waterworks involve me, and if not, go through a checklist similar to Mom and Dad's:

- You bleeding?
- Something broken that we can fix?
- Need a minute to yourself?

At which point, if they're still flooding the area, I pat their head and slink away. Giving Alice this news about her mom could help me avoid any or all of this process.

"There's something you should know." I talk fast, since the family combat may end at any minute and the distraction keeping us under the radar will be gone. "I got this message from my grandfather a day early, before any of the other tidings, something that's never happened before. But it wasn't a handwritten note; it's a cassette tape, which is totally odd and which is why the player from Thistle's was so important to me. And when I played the tape, Gumpa said it was important to your family. Then I heard this lady's voice on the other side. Your mom's voice."

"My *mom's*?" Her voice is shrill, but when I look over at my family, the balloons are still flying. Not a blip. No one heard. Alice hesitates, as if what she says will lead her to a point of no return. "What do you mean?"

I tell her the stuff she needs to know, about Gumpa's side of the cassette being garbled, about the few words I could make out. About flipping the tape over and hearing her mom introduce herself, about the start of a conversation with Gumpa. About the date, six years ago in April. About stopping before I listened to all of it.

"So you're sure it was definitely an interview?" Alice grips the metal rim of the seat back that separates us. "With my mom?"

"That's exactly what she said. And your mom did come to the island to talk to my grandfather, right?"

"Are you joking about this?"

"I wouldn't joke about something on my grandfather's tape. If he sent it to me, he wants me to see something through."

"Wow." Alice stares at me for so long I wonder if she has X-ray vision. "Can I hear it?"

"That's the idea." I glance over at the balloon fight, which apparently has come to a stop. General Mom's got each soggy twin by a sleeve. Dad and Willa are wringing out their hair. Vivien and Mr. Jones are making sure the crates filled with tidings are secure. The deliveries usually take a good hour or more. Instead of going with everyone, Alice and I could stay behind. We could go to the Fortress of No One but Me, just to be safe.

Noooooooooooo.

The little voice inside me is wailing over the prospect. I vowed long ago that no one could ever set foot in there except for Gumpa and me. None of my friends even know it exists. But sharing the cave with Alice would be helping Gumpa, wouldn't it? And me. And her.

Crud. My family's organizing. My mom's telling people what to do. I don't have much time for the little voice inside my head to get on board.

"The tape is somewhere secret," I declare, ignoring the deep bellows of protest still happening in my brain. "If I take you there, you have to promise not to say anything to anybody."

"I promise," Alice answers solemnly. "But what about the deliveries?"

"That's the tiny snag. It would be weird if you and I wanted to stay back and hang out."

"Yeah, my dad might be skeptical." She taps her fingers thoughtfully on the seat. "How about I tell my dad that the day's just been too much and I want a break? It's pretty close to the truth anyway."

Agreeing on the plan, we hop out of the golf cart and intercept Mr. Jones on his way over.

"Dad, I'm really tired. I'm not sure I'll last going around the whole town," Alice says, then explains, in a voice that's an amazing blend of exhausted and still healthy, how the day has taken its toll. "Would you mind if I stayed behind at the lighthouse?"

"Are you all right? After everything you and I talked about?" Mr. Jones looks worried. "I should take you home. Or I could call Neesha . . ."

"No, the movie's already started." Alice touches her dad's arm and smiles. Small, but reassuring. "Don't worry. I can just hang out and relax. Read books. Watch the ocean. Take it easy."

"I don't know, Alice." Mr. Jones's anxiety looms large. "No one will be here. I don't feel comfortable leaving you—"

"I can stay here, Mr. Jones," I interrupt the moment my mom wanders toward us alone, which could be good or bad timing. "Keep Alice company."

Mr. Jones's attention, which was totally directed at Alice, is now aimed at me. His face knits into a dubious frown.

"Everybody ready?" Mom asks. Mr. Jones gets Mom up to speed on Alice. And my offer.

"I am biased, but Leo's very responsible, Oliver." My mom appraises me with her ten-second, truth-or-consequences, complete-to-the-bone, this-is-going-on-your-permanent-record look. "And very trustworthy. He's never given us a reason to worry. We have a landline in the lighthouse if they need to call, but I can also give him my cell phone."

Mr. Jones agrees, though very reluctantly, going by his sharp *I'm warning you* squint targeting the spot between my eyes. I remind myself to hug Mom more.

"Can we stay, too?" Mason and Caleb appear at Mom's side like the annoying pests they are. "We don't wanna go on the deliveries either."

Oh, no. Please, Mom. Not the twins.

"Alice doesn't need to spend the rest of a challenging day chasing you two around," she replies, clucking at them. Another hug for Mom. "Let's go, boys. Into the golf cart." She pauses, with a purposeful look over her shoulder. "I don't like the clouds. Stay near the lighthouse."

"Call me if you want to go home, Alice," Mr. Jones reminds her, at the same time impaling me with his gaze again. "I'll come right back."

"I'm fine." Alice hugs him, just enough (it seems to me) for comfort. "Go and learn stuff."

Learn stuff.

About us. About the tidings.

Mr. Jones's purpose may not be to destroy the tradition, but what if Alice decides to tell him about Gumpa's tape? He certainly can't ignore that, and once his hundreds of listeners hear his story, they'll probably stampede the island, grabbing any chance to record a message for "Heaven." The lighthouse will be overrun.

Alice and I stand by while Dad and Mom load the crates into our family's cart. Mom rides with Mr. Jones. Alice and I don't say anything else until they are well down the driveway. We move a few steps to the shade near the garage.

"Just curious," I ask, trying to sound indifferent, "how many people listen to your dad's show?"

"Not exactly sure. A hundred thousand?"

My heart and stomach jerk out of my body and onto the gravel. They lie there, quivering. "You said a hundred thousand. Like a hundred people times a thousand."

"Yeah." She shrugs. "Could be a little less, but I'm pretty sure I heard him say that number before."

"Holy moly," I mutter. Not hundreds. *A hundred thousand.* Searching every square inch for a miracle. "You can't tell your dad anything—not one word—about this afternoon."

"I said I wouldn't. Besides, I could've told him everything a second ago." Alice folds her arms across her chest, but her expression seems more thoughtful than upset. "I get why you don't trust my dad, but why did you tell me about the interview at all, if you're so worried?"

Despite the sun darting in and out of the clouds, the heat is blazing through my floppy hair. Alice swipes the skin above her lip. Our valuable time is baking away in the heat.

"Gumpa trusted me," I say honestly. "And it seems like he trusted your mom."

"So what are we waiting for?" She starts walking toward the beach. "Let's go."

Alice

Rewind and Replay

Leo takes me to the massive boulders curving around the end of the beach, the ones I saw when I was walking with my dad yesterday. As we get closer, they look large, slick, and more than a bit treacherous. Of course, Leo bounds onto the first rock, a lower step to the others. With the wind whipping his hair across his eyes, he gestures for me to follow. "There's a cave. You can't see it from here."

"A cave?"

The only time I've been to a cave was when my dad took Clara and me to Luray Caverns a year or so after Mom's accident, mostly because Dad was trying to fill our days with more than old memories. But Luray Caverns is in Virginia near the Shenandoah National Park, with postcard-worthy rock teeth pointing at your head and stalactites that play music.

I glance at my feet. My flip-flops aren't the best shoes for climbing, but they do have ridged soles, and I'm not going barefoot. The wind's pushing the water against us in a heady mist, but I manage to climb up like Leo did. He tells me that even though it's low tide for another few hours, the waves are rolling in so we have to be careful. It's worth it. I'm about to hear the last words my mom might have ever uttered. I'm going to hear my mom's voice after six years. And, even crazier: What if this is some kind of sign? What if she sent it because she knew I was here? There could be clues about how to contact her.

After a minute or two of cautious footing, Leo points to a crevice between a few rocks. "The fortress is down there."

"We're going into that hole?" I ask. I was imagining we'd walk into the cave, not squeeze in and climb down.

He goes first. Then, from inside the cave, he holds his arms up to spot me. "Trust, right?"

Trust, trust . . . I slither through the opening and touch the ground with a sigh of relief. The ceiling in the cave is high enough for us to stand, but there are no pointy rock teeth and no music. It's damp and dark with shiny walls. Where a bear might live if he could handle the loud crash of the ocean. And the thick, rotten smell that's part decaying nature and part cellar.

"Welcome to the Fortress of No One but Me." Leo heads back to a rock shelf and hops up.

I hop up, too. "Like your very own Fortress of Solitude?"

"You like Superman?"

"Sorta." I tell him how Dad watches retro movies and TV shows. *Superman* from the 1970s was one of his favorites. I notice these large tubs on the ledge above us, and Leo grabs one. "What's in those?"

He sits next to me and opens the lid. "Supplies."

"Like what?"

"Snacks, drinks, clothes, survival stuff—"

"Survival stuff?"

"Gumpa taught me to be prepared. I'm going to run the lighthouse someday."

"Wow, really?"

"That's my plan." Leo grins at me. "Until then, though, this is perfect for when I want to hide out from a hurricane or my brothers and sisters for more than an hour."

I laugh. "I only have Clara, but I can see how a place like this could be handy."

He pulls a small backpack from the tub. Inside is a battered old coffee can. The coffee can he told me about. With the tape.

My heart's pumping so loud I can hear it over the waves. This is really happening.

"I'll play the B side first," he says. "Since your mom speaks on that side."

He slides the cassette into the machine and hits a button. There's static.

"Wait!" I cry, waving my hands. Leo hits STOP. "Whatever comes next, whatever I hear, whatever I find out, is huge."

"Kinda like, once we play this, everything changes?" he asks. "Like there will be a Before the Message and After the Message?"

Nodding, I drag in a ragged breath. "Right. Like Before and After my mom disappeared. Back home, my room is filled with Mom's books and notes. Ever since she died, I've been wondering what they might lead me to, wishing they'd lead me to her. And with the press of a button . . ."

I can't wait anymore. I point at Leo to hit PLAY. A voice shimmers into the air.

Anny Jones. Interviewing John Mercury [shkrrrhsh] Aviles [tk-tk-tk-tk] . . .

I lean toward the machine. I tug on Leo's arm. I'm gasping. Goose bumps on goose bumps on goose bumps. "Rewind, rewind."

He plays it again.

Anny Jones. Interviewing John Mercury [shkrrrhsh] Aviles [tk-tk-tk-tk] . . .

OhmygoshOhmygoshOhmygosh. "It's her, it's her!"

Leo presses PAUSE. I swat his shoulder, gesture every which way as if I've lost my mind. "Keep going," I say, "unpause, unpause!"

There's more static, and she says the date, six years ago.

I'm jouncing and laughing and my eyes are watering. I don't even care what she's saying. Aside from the whoosh and crackle, her melodious voice sounds exactly as I remember it: singing in our kitchen while she poured our cereal, calling my name when she picked me up from school, cooing in the circle of the night-light when she tucked me into bed. I'm hearing my mother speak as if she's right here. Right. Here. Next to me.

My heart's going:

It's Mom.

It's Mom.

It's Mom.

She's asking John Mercury a question—about when he was a boy and experienced the Great Gale firsthand. And then he starts to talk, with a voice like he's parched from the sun and as old as the ocean itself. There's so much background noise, but I can piece together that after the storm he walked home from the schoolhouse, where the smaller kids had been gathered. His mother and older brother had vanished, but his father stood in the splintered wreck of the lighthouse.

Mom asks him a few more questions, and even though it's hard to ignore the static, every word brings Technicolor to other moments, my family's moments that have faded but that I've tried not to forget.

Then John Mercury asks,

Why are you interested in this?

At first Mom reminds him about her research, but he scoffs.

Good research starts with [shhhhhkkkk] heart.

She says something I can't make out, like *Who's doing the interview here?* and we have to rewind and replay practically every other word. But for a handful of seconds, we get something amazing:

When I became a mom [ssshhhhk] first time [chchchch] the thought of someday never [whhhrrrr] able to communicate [clk-clk] daughter petrified me [zhhhrrk] want to see my children grow up and grow old. Finding [k-k-k-k-k] people have discovered an afterlife [shhhshhhhshhh] even more important.

When I became a mom for the first time.

Mom's talking about me.

That's it. I break open. Everything I've trapped tight today, yesterday, weeks ago, years ago, gushes out. Tears race down my face, tears pool in the corners of my mouth, tears salt the insides of my lips. Mom came to Aviles because she didn't want to miss a minute with her family. With me.

Now John Mercury is speaking through a series of rattles and clicks.

I understand. I have a daughter. And grandkids. And I'm dying.

Leo clears his throat, and the sound makes me jump. For a second, I forgot where I was, even forgot Leo was here. I glance over, and he's blinking like he's got sand in his eyes. The tape keeps playing. It's Mom.

You'll be able to send them messages. Think of that wonderful gift.

There's static and then he replies.

Yes, but I won't [shhhhshhhh] hold anyone's hand anymore. And they won't [ssshhskkk] hold mine.

Leo climbs down from the rock shelf and stares at the wall of the Fortress until the interview ends. I stop the tape when it finishes in a clatter of white noise, unsure what to say. Then I realize he probably wouldn't want me to say anything.

Leo

No Time to Waste

Our walk back to the lighthouse is slower, quieter. Alice and I slosh through the water, which keeps us cool and helps clear my head. Foam surges around my knees, then gets dragged back into the curl of the waves, only to disappear.

I didn't think it would be hard hearing Gumpa's voice, considering I'd heard side A before. But when he talked about how he'd miss holding someone's hand after he died, I could feel his thick square fingers wrapped around mine. I miss him so much it makes my stomach hurt.

We listened to the tape a couple times, stop and go, before we decided to head back. This whole situation, Gumpa's cassette, Alice's mom, the cryptic message, is out of a book, like finding pieces of a treasure map and not knowing how they fit or where they lead. I shared the tape with Alice, which I'm pretty sure is what Gumpa wanted, but now what? There has to be something else I need to do. Otherwise, why would Gumpa have gone through all this trouble to send a recording?

He said he wanted the Joneses to find something, and the ocean would show me. But what?

Then something hits me. "Gumpa said he wanted your family to find something. Do you think he sent this—"

"—as a clue for my family to find Mom?" Alice does this sideways hopeful-happy shuffle through the waves as she plucks the idea right outta my mind. "I was thinking the same thing. You said part of the tidings tradition was sending messages back. We could send a message to your grandfather and ask, since we couldn't hear everything he said. Send something for my mom, too?"

"It's worth a shot," I suggest, inspired by her enthusiasm. "I've never gotten a tape before this one, but maybe we could record our messages?"

"We can't record over the one we have, though," Alice points out as we climb the lighthouse dunes. "Know where we could find a blank tape?"

"There's a box of old ones in the attic we could dig through."

"Great," Alice says, and we leave our flip-flops at the back door of the lighthouse, shake off our sandy feet, and head upstairs.

"Willa and Vivien's room." I thumb toward the open door as we pass. Alice peeks in at the small pink-and-gray space as I jab toward the next room. "My room, with Mason and Caleb."

"Everything's so neat."

"That's because we each only have about six inches to

ourselves. We have to stay within the boundaries or risk plundering."

"Three of you together." She winces sympathetically. "That's rough. Clara and I share a room in the cottage we're renting, but not back home. How do you get along with your brothers and sisters?"

"Keep one eye open every second." I laugh. "Rely on yourself. And get used to being invisible."

"Oh, invisible as in when you're shouting what you think at the top of your lungs, and no one seems to hear you?"

"Bingo."

"I get that."

I point to the attic door in the hall. "The rope's a little tricky," I remark, knowing this demonstration might be more than embarrassing. Sure enough, I execute a very ineffective jump that barely brushes the rope and sends me into the wall.

"Yowch." Alice grimaces, then tries the move herself. She swings the rope enough to catch in her fingertips. She frowns. "Almost. Let me try again."

This time she gets it and pulls hard on the door. I reach up to help her ease the ladder down and climb up first. Even though it's on the small side, the backpack feels like an awkward unconscious hippo thumping heavily against my shoulders. A blast of stuffy heat whacks me in the face. "Get ready to roast. We've gotta be quick. The box of tapes is in the back."

"You're not kidding. How is everything not melting up

here?" Alice pulls her shirt away from her skin as she steps up behind me and follows me in. "Wow. You have six boxes marked *scrapbooks*. Clara and I have one box between us. Since Mom disappeared, Dad started storing our pictures on this big hard drive in his office. I wish we had more. I don't even have a good photo of Mom. Seems she was always the one taking them."

"My mom's like that, too." I go deeper into the sauna to the box where I found Gumpa's cassette player the other day. "The tapes are over here."

First, Gumpa's Spaghetti Soundtracks. No way can I record over these, but I take one out, hold it. I can hear the brassy trumpets, the sliding sax, the twirl of piano keys. I can taste the sauce, the tomato tang, meat thick as can be, fat juicy mushrooms Willa would shove to the side of her plate. The sauce would simmer for hours. My dad's sauce is from a few jars and a tiny box of wine.

I set Gumpa's tapes aside on a nearby carton.

"None of those will work?" Alice asks.

"They're tapes my grandfather listened to while he cooked. Dinner was the best on those nights. It was the only time I saw him dance." I try to mimic his stilted, old-school bopping around, but I know it doesn't come across.

Alice laughs. "Don't you wish you could download your brain sometimes so people could really see what you mean?"

"Definitely." Smiling at her, I start sorting through the tapes in the box. "I hope there's a blank one in here."

"Can I help go through them?"

With my shoulders and head halfway in the box, I grin. "Might not be room."

Alice stays next to me, peering through the clear plastic tubs towering around us. "It's hard to talk to other people about memories sometimes, isn't it?" she says after a bit. "I go to this therapist and she makes me write down my feelings. But one or two sentences aren't enough to say how much something truly means. Even a page can't. Ten pages can't." I glance over my shoulder because I hear the frustration in her voice. She smiles wryly. "I have journals full of cross-outs."

"You go to a therapist?"

"Yeah. I lose my voice every April. Completely mute. For a few days or so. It's supposedly mental, since it coincides with the anniversary of Mom's funeral. Oh, and it also happens whenever I'm around boats because of my mom's accident. The boat ride out here was a little challenging."

"How long does it last? Not being able to talk?"

"Could be several hours, could be a few days. Dr. Figg says it comes back when I'm ready."

"That's terrible. So when you lost your mom, you started losing your voice, too?"

"Pretty much." Alice sits on the edge of a nearby armchair, a faded blue tweedy thing that used to be in my room, when it was only *my* room. "When my mom disappeared, and everyone else mourned for her, I couldn't. I told my dad I thought she was alive. He felt sorry for me at first, but wanted me to move on. I didn't dare tell him everything I was reading in her research."

"After Gumpa died, I didn't talk much either," I say. Sweat is dripping from my face into the box. "No one noticed, though. The lighthouse was filled with enough noise from friends and family coming and going, and all I had to do was listen for my parents calling now and then. Bring extra chairs, microwave a casserole, keep the twins from gluing each other's hair. Oh, wait, I think—" I land on a plastic case with no writing on the white striped sleeve inside, kinda glad to veer away from the memory. Plus, I'm sure half my body weight has dripped into the tape box. "I found something."

Alice unzips the backpack, takes out the player, and I hand her the cassette. She plays a handful of seconds on the first side. Nothing. She fast-forwards—nothing. Again—nothing. She flips the tape and tries the other side. Nothing.

The hair around her face is spirally and damp. She's smiling, but with this jumbled-up look in her eyes, same as the jumbled-up feeling in my stomach.

"We can do this," she says, but I wonder if it's a question. She must wonder, too, because she says it again to be sure. This time, more firmly. "We can do this."

We. Me + Alice, a complete stranger, a *tourist*, who listens to every word. And I don't even have to shout. I grin. "No time to waste."

Alice

Return to Sender

"**Y**our turn," Leo says. His hair is scraggly and wet against his neck. If we stood next to each other in front of a mirror, I'm not sure who would win Most Bedraggled: him or me. Even that word *bedraggled*—which essentially means the worn-out way you look being dragged from your bed before you're even 10 percent ready—doesn't cover the hair knots, dirt stains, and general perspiration blob that I am.

At least now we're sitting downstairs in the kitchen, where it's a thousand degrees cooler and where we can have some warning that the crowd is coming back. Plus, we have lemonade with a ton of ice. And homemade strawberry ice pops. I downed both lemonade and ice pop in about sixty seconds. Dad called to check in a few minutes after we collapsed into chairs. I tried to sound like I was appropriately taking it easy, normal, not at all hot and jittery.

The cassette player is on the table between us. Leo already recorded his message. He had a few stops and starts, but ultimately, he tells Gumpa that my family coincidentally came to the island, and he played the message for me, but he doesn't know what else to do since the recording is tricky to hear. He asks Gumpa to send another message back as soon as possible. Especially if it's urgent. He pauses a few seconds before and after he says, "I love you," like he wants to make the words last.

It's my turn.

It's now or never.

It's gotta be perfect. I can only do this once.

"You ready?" Leo's right hand is poised over the RECORD button, while his left holds on to his ice pop, a precarious ice chunk clinging to its plastic stick for dear life.

"I don't know where to begin." My voice sounds small and shaky. My tongue is frozen.

Leo attacks what's left of his ice pop before it slips off the stick, then rolls the piece around in his mouth thoughtfully. As thoughtful as chewing can look when you have splotchy strawberry lips. "What about this: If you knew our tape would be messed up, like the tape Gumpa sent us, and only one thing you say would be heard, what would you want your mom to hear, more than anything else?"

The refrigerator gurgles through the quiet room. I look out the window at the miles of blue ocean rippling, shining, leading out to a horizon that can never really be reached.

"Okay, I'm ready," I say, realizing—when it comes right down to it—what I have to tell my mom. The most important thing of all.

Leo presses RECORD.

Deep breath in.

"Hi, Mom. It's Alice."

I stop. Leo quirks an eyebrow, silently asking if I want him to stop recording. I shake my head.

"I'm with Leo Mercury, and we got a cassette tape with an old interview on it, you with his grandfather. I was so happy to hear your voice again, even if it was from a long time ago. I know that you're out there, just like Leo's Gumpa. That's why I'm sending this. I've always known, but sometimes it got hard, believing, when everyone else is sure you're dead. When everyone else is telling me to let you go. I have a lot of questions, and I've imagined asking you all of them. But the most important thing I need to say is this: I need you to send me a message, Mom. I need you to tell me you exist somewhere, like I've always known. Please. I love you."

Leo stops the machine when I give him the signal.

"Anything else we want to say?" He lifts his shoulders to punctuate the question, and I quickly say no before I can change my mind. "Then let's get it into the coffee can and throw it back in the water."

To make sure the tape is sealed, we put it in a plastic baggie and zip it up, then inside another plastic baggie and zip that up, before plunking it into the can. Then we run down to the beach. Leo's got the can under his arm like a football. We're doing this.

The wind's pretty strong, stinging our legs with sand. "So

is there a trick to tossing it out there?" I ask when we make it to the water. "How does the ocean know what to do?"

"We all wonder that, but no one really knows." Leo gestures with the can in slo-mo, pretending to throw it hard. "You just hurl the message with all your might, and the waves take it. It disappears with a split-second shimmer."

"Shimmer?"

"Kinda like someone's throwing a handful of silver glitter onto the water and telling you the tiding's been delivered."

"Message sent!" I shift my flip-flopped feet anxiously in the sand. "So do we rock-paper-scissors to see who gets to throw it?"

Leo hesitates for a second, but nods. "Best two out of three?"

He wins: paper covering my rock.

I win: rock crushing his scissors.

Winner takes all: scissors cutting paper. I'm the scissors.

I pull my fist high-low into the gesture Clara calls her Victory of YEESSSSSS. I get to throw the can.

"Make it good," Leo encourages, but I know how much is at stake. No pressure.

He hands me the can, and I step into the water, brilliant froth curling over my toes. I heave the can as hard and as far as possible. The trajectory's fairly decent—my PE teacher would be proud.

"Nice!" Leo exclaims as the can splashes into a big wave. "Now we should see it shimmer."

A few seconds go by.

"Did I miss it?" I ask.

"I don't think so." Leo's got his hand over his eyes as if that'll make everything clearer. "But I don't see it."

I don't either. Until something rolling up into the sand a few feet to my left catches my eye. The coffee can. "Why'd it come back?" I ask, grabbing it from the water.

"I don't know." Leo takes the can. "Wind? Stronger rip current? Maybe it didn't get out far enough?"

An idea comes to me. "Could it be *me*? Because you got the message, you need to throw it? You try."

Leo wades out farther than I went, past where the waves are breaking. The water's up to his waist.

His arm whirls back, and the coffee can soars through the sunlight before falling straight into the sea. It's so bright that I can't tell if it shimmers.

"Is it gone?" I call, scanning the area in front of me, right, left.

Leo's inspecting the water, too. Then he points behind me. "Look!"

My heart sinks. The can's caught up in the foam.

I charge over to retrieve it, secure it under my arm, and hike out to Leo, bashing through small waves with my right hip. My shorts cling to my legs, weighing them down, and I'm suddenly aware that I'm not wearing a bathing suit. I hope Dad doesn't come back before I can dry off.

There's no mistaking the disappointment and confusion in Leo's eyes. I give him the can. "One more time."

He holds it over his head and launches the can so hard

he grunts. Any other time and place I might have laughed. Instead I'm sending out positive vibes, watching it sloop into the sea and disappear. We wait for the shimmer, which doesn't come.

Leo scowls at the waves, then turns around to scan the water behind us. "Not again."

The can is spinning up onto the sand.

"Oh, no," I say, and we're ramming through the waves to reach the can before the soft swirling tide can drag it out again. Leo beats me to the can by a sprint. "What do we do?"

He shrugs, trying to play it off, but he's obviously worried.

"Well, we can't give up."

"Of course not." Leo tilts his head to the side, squinting as if he's picking up some far-off signal. "Hear that?"

I angle my head like his. The ocean whooshes and surges. "Hear what?"

"Thought I heard a baby." He frowns. "Might not be, but we should go back to the house. I'm sure our time is close to running out."

"No," I say, a little too desperate, a little too whiny, but he's right. Dad will freak out if he thinks I'm playing around after saying I needed a break from the day. I apologize with a fairly weak smile. "Sorry. We're so close."

"I get it." Leo's smile matches mine as we plod back to the lighthouse, both of us kicking the sand harder than usual. "Believe me."

When we get to the back door, Leo and I listen for voices and peek through the kitchen window to see if anyone's home. "Guess your superhearing was wrong," I said after we go inside, but once we're in the kitchen, Leo freezes.

"I'm right this time. Gravel driveway. I give us about three minutes until the door blasts open." He tucks the wet coffee can into the backpack.

"We need a new plan," I note, hearing the high pitch of little-kid voices outside.

"Can you meet tomorrow?"

"Depends on my dad and family plans. What are you thinking?"

"Truthfully? I'm not." His mouth slants as if he can't muster a real grin. "I think my brain cells are busted from everything today."

"Mine, too." A few squeals and low adult voices. Getting closer. I put my hand on the backpack strap. "Would you mind if I took this with me?"

Leo looks down at the backpack like I'm gonna make it disappear in a puff of smoke, and I don't blame him. My question was unplanned, as was my bold grab. And there's no time for "rhetorical diplomacy." C+ from Ms. Rasmussen.

"I can't let my mom go—even if it's only her voice," I explain, and as the front door opens and family noise rushes in, Leo shoves the backpack at me.

"Make sure nothing happens to it," he tells me.

I slip the backpack on and swear to protect the tape machine with my life. Then I glance down at my soggy clothes. What will I tell Dad?

"Tomorrow," Leo notes in a loud voice as his brothers race

past us to the fridge with Willa at their heels, ordering them not to take the last frozen waffle.

My dad fills the doorway behind Leo's parents. He's asking how I feel. Mr. and Mrs. Mercury also check in with me, to make sure I'm okay.

"Much better." I point under my dad's arm to the lemonade glasses and plastic ice pop holders licked clean. The din in the kitchen is growing louder. The baby, on Mr. Mercury's chest, definitely wants part of the waffle action.

Dad hugs me. He's a humongous blanket of body heat, simultaneously comforting me and diagnosing me.

"You look and feel"—he pulls out of the squeeze—"soaked."

"We went for a walk on the beach, and I got caught by a big wave," I explain. "You're wet, too."

"I've been walking around in Florida summer," Dad says by way of rational explanation, and thanks the Mercurys for letting him be part of the deliveries and offers to bring breakfast or lunch for them tomorrow.

"You're coming back?" I ask, knowing I sound overly excited about the prospect. I glance over at Leo, who is pseudo-listening to his dad while eavesdropping on me and my dad.

"I learned a lot about the Mercurys during the deliveries and got a lot of good background material." He surveys the backpack across my shoulders. "You didn't bring this, did you?"

"Leo gave me a few books to borrow," I reply. Dad nods

and says goodbye to the Mercurys, enthusiastically thanking them again.

While Dad's distracted, I mouth *Tomorrow* in Leo's direction.

Tomorrow will have to work.

Leo

Coexistence Is a Mess

I'm pacing in the narrow hallway at the foot of the stairs. It's almost dusk and time for us to turn on the lantern. I can hear the twins winding down their bath upstairs. More than likely, a twin tidal wave has carried each one of their 37,000 plastic toys way over the tub. Which means an extra five minutes cleaning up the casualty zone. Tonight is Caleb's turn to flip the switch, and based on the shouts echoing through the walls, Caleb and Dad are having trouble seeing eye to eye.

With my shoulders near my ears, I keep moving. It's bad enough that living in this house is like being caught in a people tornado, but nothing else is going smoothly either. Why didn't our message sink into the water like it was supposed to? The ocean was a lot rougher this afternoon, and Mom did claim something was "brewing." And practically speaking, no one usually attempted tossing out messages during bad weather. Still.

Through the back windows, the sunset stretches its shadows down the beach and across the coquina rock. Puffy plum-colored clouds move fast across tracks of orange. I can barely make out the Fortress of No One but Me. Correction: the Fortress of No One but Me, with Special Guest Star Alice Jones.

Gumpa always talked about these old shows that had special guest stars and ended with questions like this: *Will Leo Mercury and Alice Jones figure out the mystery of the tape before Alice returns to her real life? Will Alice Jones meet her long-lost mother? Will Leo ever find out what Gumpa was trying to tell him?*

The real question on my mind: *Will Leo and Alice actually be able to send their message?* They have to.

Stay tuned.

I stop pacing in front of Gumpa's framed Rules. I read #3: *At the end of the day, be able to say you've done your absolute best.*

Have I?

"Nooo!" Caleb's whine shimmies off the walls. A strong muffled response comes from Dad. Over the horizon, the sky still streams with color, but night's taking over. Where dark blue meets streaks of rust, I see a star. The first star. Mom always says you can't waste a wish. So I wish. Hard. For so many things that they all collide with each other and nearly explode.

Then I march upstairs to see what's holding everyone up. We have to light the lantern.

Mom's in Viv and Willa's bedroom, untangling Willa's hair

and refereeing a that's-my-brush argument, and Baby Ansel's crawling toward the door with a plastic dog in his mouth. With a huff, I haul him under my arm and glance around. He waahs and thrashes against my waist. No one notices.

"Anyone going to light the lantern tonight?" I ask, not bothering to hide my irritation.

"We're getting there!" Mom calls cheerfully.

I groan. *Getting there* could last two minutes or twenty. After she finishes with Vivien and Willa, another crisis is bound to erupt between here and the light.

I kiss Baby Ansel's powdery head, set him down at Mom's feet. Through the bedroom window, the sun's mostly gone.

Time to light the way home, Gumpa used to say every night. *For those who lost track of time out on the water, who forgot about low tide and jagged rocks, who didn't check the weather before taking their boats out.*

Like Alice's mom.

Mom's *Getting there* will take too long.

I run up the tight staircase to the lantern room and into the console closet. I only let myself reconsider for a second before I flip the switch. The lens begins to turn, pouring brilliant light out into the world. The sight of it fills me. Right before I hear a herd of rhinos galloping up the steps.

"Leo! It was Caleb's turn to turn on the light," Mom says. Caleb's in his pajamas and squished in the doorway next to her. I see Dad behind her on the stairs.

"Does it matter?" I reply. "This doesn't seem to be a big deal to anyone but me."

"Leo." Mom's tone is sharp. One part angry, one part disappointed. "That's not fair."

"You should know how important this is, Mom," I say. "You told me how horrible Gumpa felt about Mrs. Jones's boat accident."

"What's with the traffic jam?" Willa calls, annoyed. She's probably halfway up the stairs, last in line. "What's going on?"

"Leo already turned on the light," Caleb reports, but I cut him off. "You just do this because Mom and Dad make you. You don't really care."

"Leo already turned the light on?" Willa exclaims. "Awwww, is he in trouble?"

"You see?" Frustration cracks through my voice. "Kid nonsense."

"Hey!" Willa and Caleb protest.

"It's a big deal to every one of us, Leo." Mom's lips fold into a dark, serious line. Her punishing tone stings. "We're the lighthouse keepers. That's why we live here. That's why my family's lived here for generations. And this *kid nonsense* is part of that family. Last I checked, you were part of that nonsense, too."

"What she said," Vivien protests from somewhere—probably a step below Dad—her voice pitching. I hear her say something, maybe to Willa, but I can't make it out.

"I'm running out of air," Mason complains, from somewhere in the stalled staircase parade.

"Okay, before someone suffocates," Dad intervenes, "let's

go downstairs and get to bed. No sense crowding up here now."

Mom turns to help him herd everyone down the steps. I should apologize, but I don't. I'm too wound up. I don't even follow them right away. And when I do, I hurtle myself downstairs and out the back door. I don't stop until I'm in the water. Up to my knees. A wave shoves a big shell into my ankle, and I reach down to grab it, hurl it away.

With every molecule in my body, I yell. About things that suck. Things that don't make sense. Things that make me super frustrated. About my brothers. About my sisters. About Gumpa.

"Can you hear me out there, Gumpa?" I holler, stomping through the waves. "What were you trying to tell me? Why couldn't we send a message back to you?"

The waves are growing massive, starting way out, farther it seems than the lantern light can reach. Each wave is bigger than the next, fighting its way to claim more and more sand. The night feels huge and dark, like it might swallow me. Like another night, not long after we moved in with Gumpa.

That night, I couldn't sleep, so I was heading for some milk in the kitchen. The back door was open. And there was Gumpa, barreling down to the ocean and shaking his fist, shouting his head off like he had the power to hold back the tide. He was practically Poseidon himself, crashing headlong into the waves, but I was scared he'd hurt himself out there. So I ran to him.

"It's too much," he roared when I got close enough to hear,

170

and threw something with all his might into the angry sea. "She shouldn't have come. I can't listen to this anymore. Take it away."

At the time, what Gumpa threw didn't seem important because I just wanted him safe. I grabbed on to him, begged him to come back to the house.

But standing in these choppy waves, thinking back to that night, I know what he threw was important. It was the cassette tape. The interview with Alice's mom. The question is, why?

Slam!

My legs buckle as a wave hits me from the side. I go down, one hand trying to brace on the sandy bottom, the other flailing out in front of me. I push my head up through the dark foam, desperately trying to regain balance. That's when I feel the arm around my waist.

"Leo!"

Dad drags me onto the beach. I'm sputtering, gasping. My throat's raw.

Dad's long hair drips into my face as he gives me the once-over. Maybe the twice-over. Patting every inch of my body, obviously trying to see if I'm hurt. Finally satisfied, he sits next to me, anchoring his arm across my shoulders. He's panting. "Did that madman stunt make you feel better?"

I'm breathing kinda hard myself. In a way, I'm glad because I don't know how to answer and it's nice not to.

"I know you're growing up," he says, "but your old dad can't go zero to sixty anymore. Can you let me know when you want to attack the world next time? I'll stretch first."

I sorta smile.

"Look, I know you bunk with two enthusiastic six-year-olds—"

"Enthusiastic?" I bark out a laugh.

"And I get that your priorities and interests are changing—"

"I'm not changing, Dad," I say. "Everyone else is."

"Is the ocean always the same?" His question blasts at me. "No."

"Neither are we." With his arm still around me, he points in front of us. "The ocean is fluid. Every second, millions of possibilities are missing one another and colliding with one another. Coexisting."

"But our coexistence is a mess."

"And it's not a mess out there?" Dad asks.

The lantern light cuts across the dark sea and back again. There's no telling the ocean from the sky.

"Every one of us loves this place," Dad says, "and we all loved Gumpa. But your mom shoulders most of the responsibility here. She thinks a lot about how not only to uphold his way, but our family's ways and the island's ways, too. She was really hurt tonight when you turned on the lantern without us."

I shiver, partially from the wind, but mostly because I know Dad's right.

"I know you may feel like you're alone like that boat out there." Dad gestures west to a single glint of light, a boat so far away I can barely make it out. "But we see you, Leo."

He unwinds his arm from my shoulder and stands. "By the

way, we decided that your brothers and sisters will choose your consequence for taking away lantern time. First thing tomorrow."

Groaning, I stand up, too. Tomorrow will be nothing but demands (from them), groveling and futile negotiation (from me). Tomorrow will be on-call diaper duty. And Mom doesn't use the plastic disposable kind of diapers. The twins will dream up any number of things for me to eat, dump over my head, or smash. Willa's been itching to get her hands on scissors and my hair. And Vivien. I don't know what to expect from her, and that's the most dangerous. Tomorrow will be lost. And there's no telling if tomorrow might stretch into the next day. When will Alice and I get another chance to send our messages? We have to find out why Gumpa sent that interview and what he wants us to do.

"C'mon. Better rest up." Dad yawns big and hikes up the sand.

Following, I look once more over my shoulder. The blip of a boat's still out there, flickering like a candle. An idea shoots through my brain like a flare.

Maybe Alice and I can use the *Buoyant*.

Alice

Why Aren't You on My Side?

Tonight, the cottage smells like home. Or more specifically, browning taco meat.

Neesha and Dad are circling the kitchen making dinner, and Clara's in the living room with headphones on, drawing on a portable easel she packed in her suitcase. I'm in the bedroom, door locked, nightstand pushed against it, suitcase wedged underneath.

Leo's cassette player's on my bed. The cassette tape is in my hands.

With my mom's voice on it.

I heard my mom's voice.

Today.

I've been debating whether to play the tape again. Part of me worries that I might accidentally break the player again, or my fingers will slip and I'll erase the messages. Either way, I'd have to explain the incident to Leo. Then he'd hate me. End of partnership. And since Leo's more likely to get to the bottom of why we couldn't send out our message, I can't let that happen.

The other part of me knows I can be careful. Really, really careful.

Knows I can keep the volume down to level one.

Knows I can put my ear right against the speaker so no one else will hear.

Just for a second.

So I do.

I breathe slowly, I move slowly. "With intention," Neesha says sometimes when she's talking about her yoga. I put the tape into the player. I press PLAY.

There Mom is again, in that voice that reminds me of classical music and storybook time when I was younger. I try to imagine how she looked when she recorded this. Was she wearing the clothes she left home in, that last day—a dark blue sweatshirt, jeans, dark blue sneakers, her coat? Her hair in a long ponytail, so straight and shiny?

"Alice! Dinner!"

I'm startled by Clara's bellow right outside the door, but I knew that someone would hunt me down eventually. I keep my cool. "I'll be there in a minute."

"Can I come in? I want to change my shirt."

"You look fine." I hurry to put away the tape and cassette player. I stumble on the bumps in the wooden floor, panicked that Clara will manage to come in and see what I'm doing. "We're eating at home. Wash it later."

"I spilled juice on it." She rattles the doorknob.

"Hey, whoa, wait!"

"Dad? Alice won't let me in!"

"Hold on." Pop tape out, put tape safely in cover. Put tape in backpack. Put cassette player in backpack. Put backpack way under dusty bed. Drag nightstand away from the door. Hurl suitcase into closet. Careful, careful, breathe, breathe. Sweat, sweat.

"What are you doing in there?"

"Nothing."

"Alice?"

Dad.

"Ready," I announce, swinging open the door and smiling at them through huffs. "Sorry. I was changing clothes, too."

Clara eagle-eyes me, then shoves past. "You were wearing that shirt before."

I roll my eyes. "Whatever."

But I'm relieved I got everything stowed away.

"Let's eat," Dad says, leading the way to the kitchen.

At dinner, Clara and Neesha talk about the movie they saw and a possible kayak trip the ticket gal at the theater mentioned. Neesha thinks would be fun for us to do before we leave. I admit it does sound pretty neat, if I'm knee-deep in the water and not in a boat. Then Dad, who's sitting next to me, starts going on about some fishing spot Mr. Mercury told him about while they were delivering the tidings. He's animated over his taco.

"Fishing, hmm?" Across the table, next to Clara, Neesha spoons homemade salsa onto her plate. "The entire time we've known each other, you've hardly ever mentioned fishing."

"Well, Elijah's caught dinner a bunch of times. Enough to feed his entire family." Dad goes on to talk about the size of the fish, the kind of pole, and other dull details that are far less important than why he was really with the Mercury family in the first place.

"What about the deliveries?" I ask. "Was it neat to be there?"

"It was." Dad takes a drink of water. "Honestly, I didn't want to focus on the tidings, and as we went door-to-door across the island, I was still wondering if this could be one big complicated scheme. But every single person on this island was so grateful to see the Mercurys coming. Though some were wary about me tagging along, a few trusted the Mercury family enough to invite me in. They even shared one or two messages with me."

It's a good thing I'm munching a particularly big mouthful of taco or this would have shot out of my mouth: *Guess what? Leo Mercury showed me a message, too. A cassette with Mom's voice on it.*

But if it had, Dad would have had too many questions. He'd want to hear the tape. He'd probably play the tape for Leo's parents. He'd pull it apart. Take the magic away. And I promised Leo my dad wouldn't find out. And Clara . . . I hate to think where things might go with her.

"That's awesome," I say when I can swallow.

"The people on this island are good people," Dad says. "And I've certainly never been in a situation where the probability of truth is zero, yet what I'm finding defies probability."

"What does all that mean?" Clara asks, but I get it. Dad's coming around!

"It's a nice idea," Neesha says, "not having to completely say goodbye to the ones you love. It's like their spirits still inhabit this space."

Clara wrinkles her face, a little creeped out. "Like some kinda ghosts?"

"In a comforting way," Neesha reassures Clara, but she doesn't look swayed.

"True," Dad says, "but people here are always thinking about what their relatives who have passed on might think. It's like the living need permission from the dead to make decisions, to change, to dream different dreams. How can they sell a shop or a house that's been in their family for years? How can they revise tradition to make it their own? How do they maintain their relationship with ghosts without becoming ghosts themselves?"

"We have a ghost in our family, too," Clara mutters, before chomping into her taco.

"Our mom is not a ghost," I shoot back.

"Girls," Dad warns. "Don't start this."

"Maybe they should hash this out, Oliver." We look at Neesha, who eyes us thoughtfully, seriously. "It might help."

Dad's expression falls somewhere between stern and unconvinced, his forkful of rice and beans in limbo. As the moment stretches out, the kitchen timer buzzes. We all jump. Dad's fork clatters to his plate, rice and beans tumbling.

"Extra taco shells." Neesha's explanation sounds like a pseudo-apology as she gets up to turn off the noise.

"You're right, Alice. Our mom's not a ghost," Clara says,

to my surprise, leaning toward us across her plate. "Neesha is our mom. I mean, she does everything for us. She fixes dinner. She comes to Muffins with Moms Day at school. She doesn't get annoyed when I need help with my math homework. She makes sure that we eat healthy even though we don't want to. She planned my birthday party last year. She cleaned up the couch when I threw up. She even took me to her office and introduced me to everyone. Neesha did all that. Not some lady I don't remember."

Neesha brings the taco shells as Clara finishes talking, but there's no doubt she heard. Yet I can't tell if she's sympathetic, embarrassed, or grateful. I have to admit, Clara's right, too.

I can make my own list, probably ten miles long, of things Neesha's done for me, things Neesha does for me. Putting smiley-face notes in my lunch box, even if I forgot it at home and she had to bring it to school on her way to work. Saying if I needed to go bra shopping, she'd take me. Talking me through friend drama over iced tea, peanut butter, and apple slices practically every day after school in the sixth grade. Convincing my dad to come here. Believing in me. Sometimes Neesha's there for me more than Dad.

But Neesha also understands what I'm trying to do, and Clara doesn't know what I know. And she does remember. Somewhere in her mind. Where the dreams came from.

As Neesha moves back to her chair, Dad touches her waist. "Neesha is the core of our family, but it's not that simple."

"Is it because you two aren't married?" Clara asks. "We're on vacation. You could get married here."

"Baby girl." Standing next to Dad, Neesha takes a deep breath and reaches for my dad's hand. "I'd love to be your mom. I'm proud when you call me your mom. I love every moment I spend taking care of you, being with you. In my heart, you and Alice are my true daughters. But if you have the chance to reconnect with the mom you lost, your real mom, if this place can bring you together, it's the chance of a lifetime."

"Didn't you hear me?" Clara pushes against the table, obviously frustrated. The glasses shake, threaten to spill. "*You're* our real mom. Why aren't you on my side?"

"We are all on the same side," Dad says. His voice is even, like he weighed it out before talking. "From what I've learned so far, the tidings are a living history for people on this island, and only on this island. The magic, the fantasy, whatever's happening, uniquely belongs to them. We're not going to find your mom here. Or anywhere else."

"What if you're wrong?" My voice is shrill, sharp, ready to shatter. "What if we get a message from her? What will you do then?"

"It won't matter to me." Clara's words feel like a slap in the face.

"Enough." Neesha holds up a hand in the space between us. Her smile is fragile and thin, like it will hardly hold up. At the same time, the steadiness in her eyes reassures me. She touches my arm first, then reaches for Clara so we're connected. "This is big stuff to deal with. I'm anxious, too. And so is your dad. But we're in this together, as a family."

"This is supposed to be a vacation," Dad adds with a weary smile. "Maybe we need a break. Get some perspective."

"Could we go to Orlando?" Clara's out of her seat and jumping on Dad. "Go to a theme park or something? Like tomorrow?"

I'm mentally yelling, NO. We can't. We can't. Not now. We're too close.

"Since there's not an official water taxi for hire any time we want," Dad says, "it might be better to wait until the road trip home for our theme park adventure. But there are some nice hiking trails along the beach, on the south side of the island. We could pack a picnic?"

Though the outing sounds nice, I can't take a break or get perspective. Not when I told Leo I'd come back tomorrow. Not with the chance it could work next time.

"You guys can hike and picnic all you want." I shove my chair back. "But I'm going to prove to everyone that Mom is out there. That we can talk to her. That she still loves us."

Then I leave, go straight to the bedroom, and lock the door. In a second, I have my mom's shell, her books, and the cassette player laid out on my bed. I need to get that message out to her some way. I need to show everyone that she's not gone for good.

Tidings

Day Two

Leo

Doing My Best

I sneak down the stairs from the lantern room, Baby Ansel strapped to my front. Despite the lighthouse being fairly tight for eight people, hide-and-seek can take a while. There are nooks and crannies, big gnarled chairs to hide under, and tiny corners to fold yourself into. I'm the seeker, but with a mini-person strapped to my back, I also have a built-in warning system. The rest of my siblings thought that would be fair.

I've been on the nonstop "lantern punishment train" since about seven o'clock this morning, after we collected the latest round of tidings from the beach. I couldn't really dwell on the fact there was nothing more from Gumpa because Willa demanded that I make her pancakes. The twins got in on that action, and soon enough pancakes for three became pancakes for eight. Make that eighty. After doing the dishes and scrubbing down the kitchen, I was the "other team" in staircase-car racing and the "Dark Force" in the ultimate paper airplane war. I won't admit—not even a whisper—that it hasn't been that bad, since I did have to clean Baby Ansel twice, from the yellow spit-up in his neck rolls to worse-colored stuff in other parts (ugh) twice. And no way will I admit that playing with my brothers and Willa is actually fun. If I did, I would never hear the end of it.

I hear faint snickering from somewhere near the bedrooms, then a "Hey, stop breathing on me! You're too close!"

I slink near the doorway to the room I share with the twins. I don't see telltale feet, arms, or hair sticking up behind the furniture. But the closet doors are suspiciously closed tight. I creep toward them. Baby Ansel gurgles, and I give him a shush.

"Gotcha!" I pounce when I open the doors, but there's giggling behind me.

"You don't *gotcha* us!"

I turn to see Willa and the twins waggling defiantly in the hallway, and when I take a step toward them, they squeal and scramble. I can't go after them very well with Baby Ansel's extra weight, but by the violent thumping on the wooden floors, they're hightailing it away.

"Don't worry, I'll get you!" I vow in my meanest voice, but I'm sorta laughing, too, and so is Baby Ansel. We're in hot pursuit. When we get to the top of the stairs, I see my brothers and sister shoving their way down, shoulder to shoulder.

Caleb knocks Mason against the wall with a heavy thud, and suddenly, above their heads, the frame that holds Gumpa's typewritten Lighthouse Keeper's Code sways dangerously.

Laughter dies in my throat. I can't let anything happen to those rules. "Hey, watch out!"

Securing Baby Ansel with one arm like a football against my chest, I pound down the steps. With my free hand, I flatten the frame against the wall before it crashes into pieces. "Game over," I announce. "Scram."

"Awwwww," the twins and Willa say in unison, but sprint away, apparently not willing to challenge me and my gritted teeth. Baby Ansel giggles, then tries to reach a chubby paw toward Gumpa's rules.

"Has anyone ever read you these?" I tap him lightly on the head and sit us on the stairs. "*Rule #1. Keep the body strong, the mind sharp, and the home clean. #2. The light of life will always burn if you believe.* And *#3. At the end of the day, be able to say you've done your absolute best.* Our grandfather wrote those. You never got to meet him."

Baby Ansel babbles in reply.

"Can you keep a secret?" I lean in toward his small ear and whisper, "I got a message from him. On a cassette tape. You don't know what that is, but I'll show you when you get older."

Baby Ansel gurgles and grabs the back of my hair.

"I'm actually supposed to do something important today," I whisper. "I'm going to meet Alice Jones, and we're going to send Gumpa a message back. Then I'll have done my absolute best."

Baby Ansel chirps with glee. I tell him how I thought about a plan all night. While everyone else makes the tidings deliveries, Alice and I will go out in the *Buoyant,* past the where the waves break, and toss Gumpa's coffee can into the sea, where it's sure to be carried away. We'll be high and dry before everyone returns.

Yanking my hair, Baby Ansel approves.

But then I remember what Alice said about losing her voice around boats. I wouldn't want that to happen. Guess I can tell her my plan, and if she doesn't want to try, I'll do it for us.

"I better go. Sounds like the perfect time to get the boat ready," I say against his soft cheek. "Listen. Everyone's doing their own thing."

Baby Ansel cocks his head as if he hears the same stillness I do. Stillness that is somehow thick with busyness.

I head for the kitchen, where Mom's at the table, a screwdriver inside the toaster. She's talked to me since last night, but definitely not like her regular-Mom self. I unhook the baby and set him on the floor. "I'm going to work on the *Buoyant,*" I say.

Mom doesn't glance up from the toaster. "Need a break after your morning, huh?"

"Something like that."

"It's not even ten thirty." She puts down the dress and picks up Baby Ansel, who's tugging at the hem of her shorts, and asks him, "Have you been a good boy for Leo today?"

He shakes his head, which makes Mom laugh. "I remember when Leo was your age. Stroller, a few toys, milk. Your dad and I knew exactly what made him happy. Now he's nearly a teenager, and the world can't move fast enough."

"Speaking of that . . ." I twitch my head in the direction of the front door and the garage.

Sighing, Mom turns her attention to me. "You're not out of the woods yet, Leo. But go on."

"Thanks, Mom." I turn to go. "What time are the Joneses coming?"

She jounces Baby Ansel on her lap. "Well, Mr. Jones called this morning. He decided to spend some time with his younger daughter today. They plan to hike around the island."

"Ohhh?" I croak out the word in multiple syllables, failing miserably to cover up my surprise. And what about Alice? Should I ask?

"Neesha's going to come with Alice, though," Mom says, dipping into my brain in that sometimes-annoying-in-this-case-awesome way she has. "I offered to make my famous chicken salad for lunch, and then they'll tag along later for the deliveries."

"Cool."

"I'm just hoping the weather holds."

I wander over to the window. The sky was slightly overcast when we gathered the tidings, but now sunshine darts between big white clouds. "It's sunny."

"For now."

I pat Baby Ansel's head and whisper goodbye. Time to get the *Buoyant* ready for her voyage. If I don't try today, I definitely won't feel like I've done my best at much of anything.

A sliver of sun cracks through the clouds as I duck out the front door and make a beeline for the garage.

Alice

The Light of Life Will Always Burn if You Believe

Neesha and my dad must've talked after Clara and I went to bed, because when I woke up this morning, Dad and Clara were gone, and Neesha was in the kitchen with coffee and a book, still in her jammies.

"Just you and me," she said. "But Mrs. Mercury invited us to lunch later at the lighthouse, which sounds lovely."

"She did?" My heart soared.

"And I didn't feel like hiking in the heat today." Neesha lifted her book. "It feels good to be lazy."

I'm sure Neesha meant it, since her office back home is always full of clients, and in her off-hours, she's always checking texts and emails. But I know she really skipped the activity to help me. None of this trip would be possible without her.

Now we're almost to the lighthouse. Backpack tight in my lap. In a golf cart getting bounced around by uneven gravel in the driveway, instead of unrolling a beach blanket on a dune and making sandcastles before unpacking sandwiches and chips. I press my hand against the pocket of my shorts, making sure the shell Mom gave me doesn't fall out. I brought it for good luck.

The golf cart jostles up and down, and Neesha and I bump shoulders. "Thank you for doing this today," I say, the words coming out more easily with a laugh. "I'm sure chicken salad and a thousand kids isn't your idea of a peaceful afternoon."

"You came a long way to be here." Smiling, she tugs at the flowered scarf tied around her hair, inching it back in place. "You have to see this through. It's important."

"Why do you say that?"

"I was a twelve-year-old girl once. With three older brothers. And a mom that needed to raise three men. Nothing I did mattered. I was practically yelling into the wind every day. But someone listened to me, paid attention to hopes I had. Dreams I had."

"Granma Addy?"

"She hated the word *impossible*." Neesha parks the golf cart near the garage. "Me too."

I stare down at the backpack. "I'm going to try and send a message to Mom today."

"I'm guessing Leo is going to help." She flicks her chin toward the front of the golf cart. Leo's standing in the doorway of the garage. "I'm glad you both are getting along better, despite the rocky start."

"Me too."

"Good luck," she says as I climb out of the cart. "I know this is a big deal."

"How come it doesn't bother you?" I ask. "All this stuff with my mom?"

"Grief doesn't just end when we want it to." She smiles. "I'll see you inside later for lunch. Be careful."

"I have a plan," Leo greets me once Neesha is inside the lighthouse. The garage smells like wet wood and a fish market when we go in. "But you might not like it."

"What is it?"

"Gumpa's rowboat. I think if we take it out past the waves, we have a good chance of—"

"We, like you and me? In that boat?" Leo had removed the tarp from the rowboat over in the corner. It's propped up on wooden stands and looks like it hasn't been painted or used in a century. While it has the space to hold us, it would never, ever, be called roomy. "That. Past the waves?"

"I know you said you lose your voice when you're on boats, and I know what happened to your mom, but I can't come up with any better solutions." Leo shuffles in the gravel. "It's seaworthy. I've checked it out. The coffee can can't possibly get pushed all the way back if we row out far enough."

My stomach begins to tighten into a familiar knot of anxiety. The boat ride to Aviles Island was fine, but did I want to chance this? My dad held tight to me then, after all. This would be me and Leo, in a shoebox boat, on the mighty ocean. Rowing "out far enough."

"What if that doesn't work?" I ask. "What if there's another reason the coffee can didn't shimmer away? It is unusual, with the cassette tape and everything."

"We won't know until we try." Leo goes over to the boat and touches the wood. I can tell he sees special something in it, the way I do with my mom's shell. "It will be okay."

"What if something happens out there?" My voice breaks. At least I still have my voice.

"We'll only be on the water a few minutes." Leo's tone is encouraging.

"Is a few like three or twenty-three?"

"I can go by myself." He eyes me with understanding, giving me an unspoken out. "If you want?"

My throat's already constricting, but when I imagine watching from the beach as he throws our messages out to Mom and his grandfather, it's impossible. "I have to be there with you."

"Then if we want to do this before lunch, we need to go now."

"Fine." My voice pushes out thin, like I'm pressing it through a colander. I clear my throat and focus. "How do we get the boat to the beach?"

Leo goes a couple steps into the shadows behind the boat and brings out a small cart. It has two wheels and silver crossbars on one end, a long handle on the other. "We can put it on this."

"Okay."

My "okay" scrapes out into a very dry "K." Leo eyes me dubiously but sympathetically. At this point, my body is one big heartbeat.

"I'm serious." Rubbing my hands on my shorts, I summon

the last ounce of confidence I have before it skitters away into the shadowy corners. "I'm with you."

Leo takes two orange life jackets from a nearby hook, gives me one, and puts one on himself. Then, after a second of what looks like thinking, he asks me for the backpack. He takes out the cassette player and the tape Gumpa sent and puts them on the worktable. Then he stuffs a red waterproof bag with a white cross printed on it into the backpack, next to the coffee can.

"Whistle, bottle of water, compass, flashlight, first-aid supplies," he explains. "I think that should do it. Just in case."

I fumble fastening my life jacket. *In case.* The stuff should make me feel better, but it only makes my mind feel like scrambled eggs. Maybe we should check in with his mom and Neesha first. No, no—they'd only stop us. Leo's right. What's a few minutes? In and out.

Leo situates the wheeled cart next to the rowboat. On the count of three, we lift it from its stands. The boat's heavier than I expect, and even though we're only moving it inches away, it takes some maneuvering. Leo's grunting, I'm grunting, but when it's finally lodged securely onto the cart, we grin like it was nothing, even though we know better. And it's only step one.

Leo reaches down for the handle to the wheeled cart. He grasps the left side, leaving me with the right, and shoulder to shoulder, we pull the boat out of the garage.

"What if someone sees us?"

"Don't worry. We'll go along the dunes, past the view from our windows."

The cart drags through the dirt and sand, and we manage to avoid a lizard scuttling out of the way. Occasionally, we have to tug harder when the wheels sink too deep and basically stop. At this point, we're both panting, and I'm glad I don't have to speak. There's a likely chance I don't have any words available anyway. I can't believe we're trying this.

Once we reach the wet sand, we heft the rowboat from the cart. Shuttling it into the water's no small feat as waves try to buckle our knees, but we manage to get the boat floating. With Leo on one side, and me on the other, we push the boat just past the break.

Leo tells me to get in first. I can't. This tiny boat will never stop the sea from spiriting us away.

"Alice?" He's trying to hold the boat steady. "I know you're scared, but we can't stand here all day."

I nod and scrabble over the side. The boat wobbles terrifyingly with my weight. I'm not sure where to sit, so I take the spot in the back, facing forward. As I wedge the backpack between my feet, Leo climbs in. Settling in his seat, his back to the ocean, he knocks against me. He mutters something under his breath. Sounds like, "No broken skull, no broken skull."

I want to ask what he means, but I don't want to hear a hollow nothing where my voice should be. It would make me even more nervous. I'm already soaked and shaking from the outside in and the inside out.

"All we have to do is get over a few waves to calmer water, drop the can, and that will be that," Leo says, taking up oars from the bottom of the boat.

That will be that. Yes. Easy.

Not. If I yell, no one will be able to hear me. It'll be this pitiful gasp of air.

"I just need to row harder," Leo says, and rows, slamming the ocean with big, broad strokes. We get hit by the first big wave.

The boat tilts wickedly, and I grip the seat as tightly as I can. The rush of stinging salt steals my breath as I'm rocked in the face with water. I'm sputtering, shivering, scolding myself for getting in this boat at all. By the time I recover, with half the ocean in my right ear, the boat's surging back to shore. Leo's shaking water from his ear, too. This wasn't a good idea, but there's no going back now.

The boat drifts sideways. A gigantic wave is aiming for us. It's only a second before we're being sucked into the wave's massive curve. Leo's rowing, rowing, then we're cresting, cresting, and suddenly we've got air. He's yelling, and I'm—

Whack! The boat slams back down. *Holey moley.* But Leo still has the oars. We're still in our seats. We're still okay. We're still—

"Here we go again," Leo calls, and we're driving into another humongous wave. Row, row. He's doing it. Up-up-up!
Wham.

I pitch halfway over the side of the boat. Leo snags the back of my life jacket and yanks me toward him. The rowboat surges and heaves. I'm breathless and drenched, my ponytail slogging around my neck like seaweed. Is this how Mom felt when she . . . when she . . .

"Another one!" Leo shouts. "Watch out!"

The boat manages to attack another wave without dumping either one of us into the sea. When we're steady, it begins to drizzle.

"We're out far enough to throw the can in," Leo says. "I'll keep us upright."

Given our bad luck on the shore, I wonder if he should do the honors, but we don't have time for discussion. I dig the coffee can out of the backpack, anxious to launch our messages and return to the lighthouse. Without sparing a second, I hurl the can as far as possible. It glides through the air, drops, and whops into the water.

"Can you see where it went?" he asks. "Did it shimmer?"

I squint into the waves to find the coffee can rising and falling, but before I can get too worried, it happens. The shimmer. Like some invisible hand dusting a cake with golden sugar, this magical, wondrous shimmer gathers Gumpa's can into the water and draws it from sight.

"I did it!" I raise my arms above my head in triumph. "I sent the tidings! I sent a message to my mother!"

"You did!" Leo hollers. "And you're even talking, too!"

"I am! *I am!*"

Leo's whooping, and I'm whooping, so we're not prepared when a sudden burst of lightning slices the sky. We flinch, hunch, heads into our shoulders. The drizzle has become a downpour. The ocean's shoving the boat, urging us to go before we capsize.

Leo starts to row. My body quakes. Every direction is gray. Water churns across the bottom of the boat, my legs and feet ice-cold. I notice that one of my flip-flops is missing.

Crack! I flinch as the sky floods with brilliant white light. A mammoth wave barrels toward us, its underside golden and sparkling. It's so beautiful and so terrifying, and all I can do is watch it pick us up.

We tilt. I fall from my seat, and down past Leo, past his mouth widening in a big NO, past his outstretched hand. Then my head and shoulders strike the front of the boat, and I fall partway over the side. Water's rushing around my head. My ears, nose, mouth are being thrashed with ocean. I think my life jacket might be caught on something.

Leo's shouting, "Hold on!"

I can't obey. The waves are powerful. I can't pull myself up. My arms can't fight the tide around me. I suddenly don't remember where I am, why I'm all alone in the sea. Oh yes, my mother. I was trying to send a message to my mother. Did Mom think it was worth it, coming to Aviles Island, risking everything to hold on to *forever*? Did she think forever would come like this? On a boat in the middle of a storm? All I want is to curl into a ball.

You'll be okay. I'll get you home.

Home, yes. The voice is lulling, nurturing. I don't feel the waves anymore. I'm floating, a loose ribbon going up and down. *I want to go home.*

Open your eyes, Alice.

It's hard. The sting of the salt water has made them raw, puffy. *I can't.*

You have to.

I know that voice. I open my eyes wide enough to see a blurred someone, someone who looks like—

Mom.

In the pale blue shirt she wore that day on the beach when she played with Clara and me. Hair blond and messy, as if she's about to make breakfast and needs to pull it up, out of the way. Her skin is iridescent, like something from a dream.

My entire body bursts with joy. Mom's with me—and I know she can make everything better. She'll finally answer every crossed-out question I've ever had. She'll finally tell me where she's been and prove to everyone that she's never been far away from us. I was right.

I'm throwing myself into her arms. *I found you, I found you! Everything that my heart could imagine came true.*

Alice.

Her crestfallen tone makes me pause. That's when I realize we're not actually hugging. There's something soft, firm, and invisible in the way. I squeeze her harder, but still don't feel her.

I'm sorry, she says simply. *Some things can't be done, Alice.*

I try to take her hand, not wanting her to be sorry. Not wanting her to give up. The wall between us remains.

It's all right, Mom. You got my message and that's what matters. I can contact you now, and you can contact me. Just like Leo and his grandfather.

I'm afraid not. The people of Aviles Island are part of something extraordinary. Something for them alone.

But it can't be. I'm talking with you now. I heard your interview with John Mercury. This was your research. That's why you came to the island. To be a part of it. To find a way to be with us forever.

Her smile is radiant, gentle. *Forever is making every second a lifetime of love, Alice. You have forever ahead of you. And this time is a gift.*

What about Dad and Clara? They need to know you're here.

You need to know they love you more than anything. She brushes my hair back from my face, but I can't feel it. *They're waiting for you at home.*

And I've been waiting for this moment. I grab her arm, but this time my hand slides through to water. I try to touch her arm, her cheek. More water. *Mom, I can't lose you again.*

I love you, Alice, she says, fading away. *And don't worry. There's no need to search for me. I'm there, in everything that makes you happy. I've been there all along.*

Mom, don't go. I'm flailing, trying to grasp any part of her I can. *Not after what I went through to get here. I love you, too.*

But she's gone, and I'm alone, in a hard storm of tears I'll most likely drown in.

No. Not tears. Waves. Racking my body.

Something's tugging hard at my back, pulling, pulling.

Leo.

Leo

A Legacy of Caring

Once I asked Gumpa if he was ever afraid. He said plenty of times. Yet in the stories he told, whether he faced brigands or bullies, on the shore or on ships, he always had his wits. My wits jumped ship a while back.

"Alice." I'm yanking frantically on the lower strap of her life jacket, which is caught on a piece of the prow. Her right arm and shoulder are dragging in the water, her head bobbing alongside. Waves pummel the sides of her face. "You have to help me."

I can't lose her, not when coming out here was my idea, not when I promised her it would be okay. But my arms are about to fall off, and the boat is bucking without us rowing, and if I actually stop to think, I could throw up. It feels like hours since we left the beach. It feels like hours since we've been fighting to stay afloat. I can't do this alone.

I pull and pull on the strap. She's muttering something, her eyelids fluttering. "Alice! Can you hear me?" I shout.

Lightning blinds the sky, and my head sinks into my neck turtle-style. I wait for the thunder. Mom taught me that if you count the number of seconds between flash and boom, then divide by five, you can tell how far away the lightning really is. Five seconds is a mile.

One Mississippi, two Mississippi, three Mississippi . . . *Boom*. My teeth rattle. Gumpa said the one thing he'd miss after he died was holding someone's hand. I don't want to die. I know I'm twelve, but I wish my parents were here. I wish I could hold their hands right now. They'd yell at me for being out here, but then they'd take care of everything.

Desperate, I tug the strap with all my might and finally it gives way. The force sends Alice toward me, and we both land in the bottom of the boat. Water heaves over the sides. Even though it's basically a bathtub on its way to filling up, I'm amazed the *Buoyant* is still going strong.

Alice is coughing, stammering. "I saw my mom."

Did I hear her right? "Your mom?"

Bobbing her head, she sputters. "I don't know how, but I did."

I want to say that she was probably dreaming when she went over the side, but there's something about this crazy storm, something in her voice, her voice that never went away, that tells me I have to believe her.

I can't think too much more as the *Buoyant* struggles against the wind and current. Another strobe of lightning bursts around us. One Mississippi, two Mississippi, thr—
Boom.

Alice and I both shriek. Lightning flares again. As soon as I begin to count, it flashes once more, this time across our path. I squint through the downpour.

Please . . . let it be—

"It's the lantern!" Alice cries behind me, as land, and the shape of the lighthouse, come into view.

I take up the oars and row like sea monsters are after us, but it's like the *Buoyant* knows how close we are. It miraculously rides the swells fast and forward as if wind and rain don't matter. I can see the beach, dotted with people. Some are charging into the water. Mom. Neesha. Dad. My brothers and sisters. A few neighbors from down the road. They're shouting at us. Waving their arms.

Mom's almost to us. It's like she has a machete bashing through the waves. Neesha and Dad are right behind.

"Alice! Leo! Areyouokay? Areyouokay?" they say when we get closer.

They grab the rope at the front of the boat and brace it, touching our shoulders and our faces, making sure we're whole before leading us to the beach. When we get to the shore, they help us onto the sand, squeeze us so tightly that it's almost painful, cry so much that they're practically choking. There are so many questions, and I'm glad no one waits for answers.

For the first time, as my brothers and sisters swallow me in their mess of wild cheers and squeals, I'm happy they take all the words so I can't get any in edgewise. We almost drowned. Anything I say might come out a squeak.

In the kitchen, we're bombarded by fresh clothes, mugs of hot tea, and thick towels toasty from the dryer. My mom gave Alice my old Green Lantern sweatshirt to wear to warm up, and her hair has dried a little, frizzing like seagrass in every direction. Neesha hasn't left her side for a second. I guess she called Alice's dad, and now that the storm has subsided some, he and Clara are on their way back from the other side of the island, where they had holed up in the diner to wait out the weather. My siblings bring in a board game to play. After everything that's happened, it seems like they want to stick close to me.

Alice's eyes are as big as moons, like she's trying to make sense of too many things at once. I wish we could get away into another room so I could talk to her about seeing her mom. But my mom is sitting with me on one side of the table, and Alice and Neesha are on the other side.

"We called and called you for lunch, and when you didn't come in, Neesha and I searched for you everywhere." Mom's voice is scratchy. "When we couldn't find you, I called the neighbors. Everyone was frightened to death."

"I'm sorry." The words don't sound right. They're not enough. They swell in my throat.

"You know better than to go out in a boat without an adult." I can't tell if she's mad, sad, or both at the same time. "You put Alice's life and your life at risk. For what?"

"It was my idea, Mrs. Mercury," Alice interjects. "We were sending a message to my mom."

"Your mom?" she asks.

"And Gumpa," I add.

"I assumed you were just going to toss the message from the beach. I never dreamed you'd get in a boat." Neesha's face is pale, her words stretching thin and slow like a rubber band. "I trusted you to be safe."

"*We* trusted you to be safe." Mom pounds the table softly with her fist. "And the weather, Leo. I kept telling you it would change."

"I didn't think—" I try again, but Mom stops me.

"You couldn't have thrown it out from the shore, like we always do? Or waited until tomorrow? The next day?"

I start to tell her how the message kept coming back every time, and Alice jumps in too, but Mom's not ready to listen to us right now. Maybe she'd listen to Gumpa.

"Be right back," I say, getting up from the table. I tear through the lighthouse and out to the garage. In a minute, I'm back with the cassette player and the tiding Gumpa sent me.

"Gumpa sent me a tape," I say, setting the machine and the cassette tape, in its plastic case, on the table. My dad and my siblings gather behind us.

I explain how I found the recording in a coffee can addressed to me. How one side was hard to hear and the other was an interview with Alice's mom from six years ago. Then Alice chimes in, saying how she wanted to find her mom and that the interview might've been a key. That the interview might've meant her mom is out there like Gumpa.

I'm not sure who looks more shell-shocked or tearful: Mom, Dad, or Neesha.

"Nothing like this has ever happened before," Mom says. She takes the tape out of its case, slides it into the player, and presses PLAY.

"It's kinda hard to hear," I warn.

Mom leans her head toward the machine as the static whooshes in. When Gumpa's voice comes in and out, she sits back, startled. As whirring and shooshing cut through his words, she stops the tape, rewinds, fast-forwards, and rewinds again. Mason and Willa boo at the interruption, but Mom looks serious, like she's fixed a broken tape before. But Gumpa's voice doesn't come through any clearer when she tries it again.

"He mentions the Jones family," I say. "Listen."

"This is phenomenal," Dad breathes over my shoulder. "And you said there's an interview with Alice's mom on the other side?"

Mom lets Gumpa's side go to a string of ticks, then silence before she turns the tape over. There's a knock at the front door, and she tells Vivien to go answer it as the tape begins again.

Alice's mom starts talking, just like Alice and I heard before. Mom and Dad exchange incredulous looks, and Neesha reaches out for Alice's hand. I hear something through the loud crackling that Alice and I couldn't make out before.

Tell me what you do, Mr. Mercury.

Then Gumpa, between bouts of white noise.

A lighthouse keeper's job is to look after others and bring them home safe.

Ah, a legacy of caring.

That's when Mr. Jones and Clara walk into the kitchen.

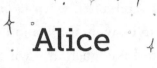

Alice

It's Hard to Say

After lunch yesterday, I didn't think Leo's family could ever be so quiet. But when my dad and Clara walk into the kitchen, no one makes a peep. My mother's voice fills the room until Leo's mom stops the tape. Dad's frozen by the fridge. Clara's hand clasps her throat like her heart might jump out. Everybody stares.

It's not until I run over to hug Dad tight, until Neesha comes over and puts her arms around us both, until Clara wriggles under our tangle of bodies and squishes in, that his shoulders start to tremble. That his face crumples.

"I'm so glad you're safe, Ali," he says, and I don't want him to let me go. "I am so glad you're safe."

Mr. Mercury herds Leo's brothers and sisters out of the room. They brush past us with hushed footsteps. One of the twins whispers, "Why do we have to go upstairs and why are they so sad?" Then the other twin whispers back, "Leo and Alice survived an adventure."

"An adventure is a mild way to describe the day so far." Dad pulls away from us, swiping his face with the heels of his hands. He's ruddy and dazed when he looks at me. "When the storm began to blow in, Clara and I changed our picnic plans and went to have lunch in town. Imagine our shock when Neesha called and said you were out in a boat with Leo. A boat. In this weather. That doesn't sound like something you'd do."

"Leo found a cassette tape." Mrs. Mercury quickly apologizes for Leo's reckless and foolish behavior, then tells Dad about Gumpa's message and the interview with Mom. "That's what you heard when you walked in."

"What?" Dad puts a hand to his forehead. "An interview with your mom? From years ago? Why would it appear now? That doesn't make sense."

"It's Mom's interview with John Mercury," I say. "The reason she came to the island."

Dad gapes at me, attempting to process.

"It's new to me, too," Mrs. Mercury says to him, walking toward the counter. "How about I put on some coffee?"

"Thank you." Dad gives her one of those kind smiles that adults use when they want to be polite but need to get out fast. "But we should go."

"Go?" I ask, my chest tight. "You could at least listen to the tape. Aren't you curious?"

"I'm a lot of things right now, Alice. Relieved, grateful, exhausted, confused, angry. Curious is pretty far down on the list." Dad puts his hand on my shoulder, and I feel him sigh.

"I'd rather listen another time, when I can think about this logically."

"You don't want to listen." I move back toward the table, Leo, and the cassette player. "It's in the past."

"Alice." There's a tautness to Neesha's voice, as if she's doing her best to smooth everything out on the inside. "We do need time to listen to one another. But you went too far today."

But I had to go that far, to find my mother. And I did find her.

As my dad expresses his gratitude to the Mercurys one more time, Leo and I say goodbye awkwardly, raising our hands, but not moving. *See ya.* I feel jumbled up. I don't want to go. I want to sit down with Leo and replay every second, making sure I don't forget any part of what we went through. But everyone else wants this wrapped up and ended.

"I wish we could talk about what happened out there," I say to Leo. He glances at our parents, who are still talking. Clara's hanging behind Neesha, big-eyed and waiting.

"The whole thing was surreal," he says, lowering his voice. "You said you saw your mom. What was it like?"

I take a step closer to him so I can whisper. "You know how the storm pretty much turned us inside out until we didn't know which way was up or down? It felt like that at first, but then I heard her voice and saw her, and for a second, it was peaceful. Until she faded away."

"That's intense," Leo breathes. "And your voice. Seems like you never lost it."

My voice. There's been so much going on I haven't really thought about it too much. But Leo's right—I can talk. During and after a boat ride that would make paddleboating seem like taking a nap.

"Think it's because you finally saw her?" he asks.

I'm about to answer when Dad and Neesha usher me and Clara out the front door and into our golf cart, its plastic sides zipped closed against the rain. The quiet vibrates around us as we bump across the gravel. All I wanted when I was on that terrifying boat was to be with my family, and now each of them seems some place faraway, in their own space, too tired, too angry, and, ironically, too tense to talk.

Clara's next to me in the back seat. Usually, we touch each other to be annoying, but now her left knee leans heavily against my right. On purpose. I thought for sure she would've said something snarky by now. Or complained that I cut her time with Dad short. Instead, she's staring out the window at the rain and the empty street.

Up front, Dad's driving. He's holding Neesha's hand between the seats. Both seem lost in their own thoughts, too.

I need to break the silence since I'm the one who caused it in the first place. "I'm sorry."

My dad clears this throat, and I'm ready for what he hasn't said yet. For what's hanging in the air.

"You're afraid of boats," he says. "You practically lose your voice even thinking about boats."

He slows the golf cart and steers us onto the side of the

road. When he parks, he sags forward. His big shoulders shudder. He's sobbing. "I listen, Ali. I hear you. Today and every day. And like your mom, when you get something in your mind, nothing can stop you. Not even me."

I squish into the skinny space between the front and back seats to hug him. Neesha rests her head on my shoulder.

"I was devastated when I couldn't find your mom," Dad says when he regains his composure. He sits up straight in his seat, and so do we. "When Neesha called me today, I was so frightened. It felt like I was reliving the worst moment of my life. I felt helpless. Even if we could borrow someone's golf cart, the storm was too dangerous for me and Clara to risk driving to the lighthouse. Neesha and Leo's parents were making all the necessary phone calls. All I could do was watch the lightning and pray you were okay."

"Dad . . ."

He wipes his eyes. "You believed in your mom, and I took that away by holding on too tightly to the past, too tightly to my own way of grieving. That's why this happened."

I'm bawling now, too.

Neesha reaches down to open her purse. "Here, take this."

She hands me a handkerchief to wipe the tears from my face. It's Granma Addy's. I touch the soft fabric to my cheek. Even now, when I ran off and didn't tell Neesha where I was going, when I broke her trust, she's still here. She's been here. She's been helping me find my mother, by being all the things a mother is. And not asking for anything in return. She has simply loved me and Clara. No matter what.

I angle my body to give Neesha a weird, slanty hug, the best I can in a golf cart. She squeezes me back, tight and warm.

"I love you, Alice."

"I love you, too."

From behind us, there's a squeaking noise. I pull back into my seat. With one finger, Clara is drawing a frowny face on the steamed plastic window.

"You haven't said a word since we left the diner," Dad says to her.

Clara erases the frown and scribbles words on the window. *Never mind.*

"Clara." Dad's smile is patient, but strained. "We're wiped out."

Clara's face reddens. She angrily swipes at her words, then turns away from us with a dark scowl. I catch a glimpse of tears in her eyes. My sister doesn't cry. At least not in front of anyone, especially me.

"Let's get some air in here." Neesha unzips her side of the plastic. For the first time since we arrived on the island, the breeze is cool and fresh. It has stopped raining. Dad restarts the cart, and we're on the road again.

I gaze at Clara, debating whether to touch her, debating whether I should do something. When I finally decide, she moves her leg away from my hand.

For the rest of the drive, the only sound is the hum of the cart, the crunch of tires on the road. Even though I'm safely on land and even though my family's surrounding me and

Dad and Neesha seem to understand, I feel like I'm alone at sea. I can't even reach out for Mom.

Suddenly, I remember my mom's shell tucked into the pocket of my shorts. With a hasty pat, I feel its hard shape like a knot way down near the seam. At least I didn't lose that.

Leo

Not My Story to Tell

For the first time, Mom delivers the tidings by herself. Dad offers to go instead, but she insists. "They're late getting out to town as it is," she says, unhooking her floppy red hat from the wall near the fridge. It stopped raining, but the clouds are lingering. "Better if I go myself and explain. Anyway, making pizza is your thing."

"Pizza?" Willa chirps from the parlor, where my sisters are playing with Baby Ansel. But I'm only half paying attention. Any other time there was an errand away from home—the supermarket, the nursery for seedlings, the hardware store, the tidings—Mom would've asked me to go. Asked me to help.

"I can come," I say as she folds up a scrap of paper and tucks it into the pocket of her shorts. I push my chair back from the table. "Unload the wagons, carry the heavy stuff."

Mom kisses me on the forehead. "Back soon."

"Really, Mom." I follow her to the front door. "I—"

She pats me on the cheek. "I appreciate it, but I'd feel better if you stayed here."

I watch her golf cart drive away, then turn back to the kitchen. Despite its warm glow, and Dad banging through cabinets as he finds ingredients for pizza, the room feels empty.

I hover near the sink until it's obvious Dad's got everything under control, then amble my way into the parlor. Willa and Vivien have Baby Ansel on the floor in a plastic green seat, and they're rolling zoo animal cars back and forth with him.

My insides are fidgety, like I'm one of those twitchy sandpipers flitting along the beach. I wander over to the fireplace that we never use and fiddle with the brass handbell and the nautical spyglass before flopping into Gumpa's leather captain's chair, one leg pumping over the side. Maybe it's the *what now?* that's making me antsy. We sent the tidings. We braved the ocean. Our parents are upset. Alice told me she saw her mom. Now I'm just waiting, and I don't know what for. Tomorrow is the last day of the tidings until next year.

The announcer from Gumpa's old TV shows chimes through my head again. *Will Gumpa write back by tomorrow? Will I ever know if I did what he needed me to do? Will I get to see Alice again?* Her dad might be too mad to come back.

"Hey, Leo." Mason and Caleb appear in the doorway. Twin expressions of uncertainty.

Yellow alert. "What's up?"

They exchange dubious glances. Caleb chucks Mason's shoulder.

"O-kayy," Mason grumbles, then turns to me. "Can you tell us what it was like?"

"What *what* was like?"

"Being out there," Mason says.

"In the storm," Caleb adds, his eyes huge. "It must've been awesome."

Mason's nodding. "Like a movie."

I blink. The twins are looking at me with an admiration I have never seen before. It's weird. It's cool. It's a first. They settle cross-legged on the floor at my feet.

"Was it scary?" Willa's chiming in now. She's scooting closer to my chair. "Did you almost drown?"

"I want to know about the tape," Vivien says. "Start at the beginning."

Let's start at the beginning. That's what Gumpa would say each time he was ready to tell us a tale. But this time my brothers and sisters are looking at me with interest and lots of expectation, even Viv with one raised eyebrow. They're admiring me. Me. They want me to tell them my story.

"Well, it began the day before yesterday." My heart's beating fast. What's crazy is I'm nervous. I don't feel awesome, like Gumpa when he was young, conquering some foe and surviving. I lick my lips. They're dried and cracked from way too much salt water, wind, and rain.

"Go on," Caleb urges.

They're waiting with grins. Even Baby Ansel is raptly studying me over the zoo animal car he's chewing. I feel like I should be larger than life right now, a save-the-day hero, not some character with loose ends to tie up. But they're listening. Each one of them. To me. And as much as I've wanted this, it makes me want to know something, something I've wanted to know since Alice and I got off the *Buoyant*.

"Before I get too far in," I say, "whose idea was it to turn on the lantern light?"

There's a burst of laughter and then a noisy, "Ours!"

When the chatter dies down, Vivien leads into how she had just set the table, and Mom had asked Willa to call Alice and me in from the beach. Willa takes over the story then. "I told her I didn't see either of you on the beach. That's when Mom and Neesha ran out and found tracks from the boat cart leading to the water."

"So we decided to turn on the lantern because it was so dark with the storm clouds," Caleb points out, and Mason picks up the idea. "Because Mom, Dad, and Neesha were busy figuring out what else to do."

"There was a little more to it," Viv admits wryly. "Dad was making phone calls to the neighbors, while Mom and Neesha were scoping every inch of the beach."

"In case you two rolled up onshore dead," Mason interrupts with more enthusiasm than necessary. Viv flicks his ear, and he yelps.

Willa cuts in. "We wanted to do something, too, and somehow we ended up on the stairs with the same idea—"

"—about turning on the lantern," Vivien finishes. "Only it took us a few minutes to decide who would turn it on."

I chuckle, imagining the deafening standoff. "So what happened?"

"I came up with an idea," Viv says.

"We put our hands together," Willa notes with her evil eye, "and turned it on."

Caleb reaches out, fingers splayed, beast-style. "One big paw, like a yeti."

He waves his hand for everyone to reenact the scene. Vivien takes Baby Ansel out of his chair and brings him over to the group. Then they put hand over hand, over hand, over hand, over hand. Oldest to youngest, with the baby's chubby hand on top. It's impossible to think, but those hands—my brothers' and sisters' hands—brought some much-needed hope to me and Alice. I wish I was there to see it. "Cool."

"I second that. You can do amazing things when you work with one another." Dad's leaning in the doorway, listening. With a grin, he claps twice. "Now go wash those hands for dinner."

"We didn't even get to hear Leo's story," Mason moans.

"Think of it as an opportunity for exciting dinner conversation." Dad ushers everybody out but me. Then he wraps me in a hug, more firm than usual.

"This doesn't mean I'm not upset with you." He lets go, only to brace my shoulders with his hands, leaning close so we're eye to eye. "It means I'm making sure you're really alive. And making sure you know for the second—and I hope the very last—time that you are not alone. Did you not understand what I said about coexistence?"

"I didn't want anyone else to . . ."

"Get their sticky fingers on Gumpa's message?"

I nod, smiling weakly.

"And if you told your mom and me, you think we would've taken over?"

"Yeah. Or nothing would have happened. It would have gotten lost in everything else around here."

"I know you're twelve. But you're right, we wouldn't have let you get in a boat *in a storm,* not to mention risk your life and someone else's to send that message. However, we might've come up with some smart, or at least interesting, ideas if you had given us the chance. You saw what those sticky fingers can do."

Beeeep. "Dad," Willa calls. "Pizza's done."

"We should make our own Rule #4 for the Lighthouse Keeper's Code. *Family means no one is ever completely at sea.*" Dad shakes my shoulders playfully, but his expression is strictly business. "If you're feeling that out of sorts again, tell me, okay?"

The oven beeps again.

Dad gives me one more shake, then goes toward the beeping. I watch as he gets the twins to find dinner plates, swoops a wiggly Baby Ansel from Vivien's arms, and turns off the oven. I meet him with a pot holder. Even though I'm happy to be on solid ground, I still feel like I'm adrift.

Alice

Pretty Lucky

No one has the energy to talk at dinner. The four of us dive into our take-out fried chicken and mashed potatoes like they are the only things we can count on. Even Neesha, who normally saves the day with some kind of positive comment or idea, just keeps topping up her iced tea.

After Dad tells us to clear the table, we cluster in the living room and zone out on a black-and-white movie, one Neesha told us about a long time ago but we never got around to seeing. But when the movie's over, by the looks on everyone's faces, I don't think any of us actually paid any attention to it. We say good night with tight hugs but not many words. Clara still hasn't said anything. Any other time, I might have felt annoyed, like she's mocking the way I go mute. I can't believe it myself, but tonight I actually just wish she'd make a joke or whine to get her way.

It takes me a long time not to fall asleep. About a thousand tosses and a thousand more turns. Tomorrow I don't want us to keep acting like there are force fields between us, yet what can I do? I think of session after session with Dr. Figg, the questions she would ask, but none of them have the power to turn us back to normal. At the same time, I wonder what normal is.

I stare at the ceiling, even though there's nothing to see but dark. I've spent years fighting to keep Mom as alive in my life as she could be. I've surrounded myself with her words, clung to every morsel of memory, insisted that everyone else was wrong to the point that my voice gave out. No one wanted to listen anymore, anyway. Is that what I want normal to be?

I roll onto my side, every lump in the mattress making me more aware of reality. I found Mom. I got to talk to her one more time, in some in-between space. But she could never have come home, no matter what stories she told herself or what stories I told myself. No matter what stories she followed around the world. Yet those stories brought her to Aviles Island, to John Mercury, to Leo, and eventually to me. Wherever Mom is, she isn't lost anymore. She just can't be with us.

At least we have a recording of her voice, which I so want Dad to play.

"Alice, Alice!"

I open my eyes wide, startled by Clara's moaning. She's sitting up in bed, head in her hands. Crying so hard I can see her body rocking in the shadows.

I'm out of bed in an instant, my arms curling around her. "You're dreaming," I whisper, and to my surprise, she burrows into me as if I can stop the tears.

"I don't . . . want to dream about . . . about her." Clara hiccups through the words. "But I do, I do. And this time you were with her. In a sailboat."

I rub her back, afraid anything I say will break this fragile moment, will make her run from me and lock everything inside again. Clara stumbles through her nightmare, describing how Mom and I tried to challenge the ocean, but the boat flipped over, and we spiraled down, down, down to the dark bottom.

"There was nothing but black and more black, Alice." Clara draws away from me, swiping her face fiercely. "I don't remember her like you do. And if I do remember, it's like this. Usually Mom doesn't even have a face in my dreams. It scares me."

"I didn't know." Her confession punches me hard. If I'd had nightmares like that since I was little, maybe I wouldn't have wanted to think about Mom either. Or acknowledge her.

Snuffling, Clara glances over at my stack of books on our nightstand. "You've always been so close to her. Reading her books and her notes. Thinking she was alive. I wanted to be like you. But I couldn't. And you make it seem like the only thing important in this family is her. You even lose your voice because of her."

"I don't mean to do that."

"I know. But it *felt* like that. It felt like because I didn't want to remember her, or call her my mom, that I wasn't good enough to be your sister anymore." Clara's voice breaks. "You almost drowned today when you were out on that boat. I thought I'd lost you for real."

My heart fractures into thousands of pieces. I've spent so much time trying not to lose Mom that Clara's been petrified of losing me. "Oh, Clara."

"I even prayed in the golf cart on the way back to the lighthouse. And the only time I can barcly remember something like that was when she . . . she . . . died and all those people were praying for her in that church. So since everyone on this island talks to people who are dead, and since you came here to find her, I thought I should pray to her. To send you home."

I don't remember when I started crying, but I am, big salty tears I can taste. Clara reached out to Mom. Prayed to Mom. Mom, who wasn't even real to her. Clara did that. For me.

I hug her again, because this time I feel like I'm the one washing away. "Thank you," I say. "And we are sisters. Nothing can take that away."

We sniffle at the same time, laughing at the snorty sound as we pull back from each other.

"Maybe you can tell me some things about her," Clara suggests. "Little by little. Then the awful dreams might stop?"

"Sure," I say. "You could hear her voice, too. On the tape."

Clara shrugs. She doesn't say no, but she doesn't say yes either.

My stomach rumbles.

"Cereal?" Clara suggests with a faint, hopeful smile, and I agree.

We fill bowls as quietly as we can and nestle on the couch, flipping through channels and landing on a movie Neesha owns at home and has made us watch seventeen times, *The Wizard of Oz*.

"We used to be so creeped out by the Wicked Witch's green face," I say, "until Neesha made Dad dress up like Frankenstein for Halloween."

"She let us do his makeup," Clara adds, and we laugh, but not too loudly.

"I don't know what we'd do without her," I tell her. "We're pretty lucky."

"You know who else is lucky?" Clara whispers.

"Mmm?"

"The people here on this island, like the Mercurys."

I look at her through the silvery shadows, surprised. "What makes you say that?"

"I couldn't imagine what I'd do if something happened to you. *Really* happened. And here on Aviles Island, people are never gone for good. That's pretty lucky."

I look at my sister. I want to ask, *Who are you?* but I don't. We're moving into new territory, and I'm not going to trample it. I do get an idea.

"I'll be back," I whisper, and tiptoe to our room. When I return to the couch, I hand her the rolled-up socks I keep under my pillow. "I want you to have this."

Clara scrunches her nose. "Your old socks?"

"What's inside."

She unrolls the ball. Mom's shell tumbles into her lap. I'd put it back when I got home from the lighthouse.

"Mom gave it to me when I was small," I say quickly, "but

I've kept it ever since. I want you to have it. To remind you that I'll never be gone for good either."

She stares at it, this small pink-and-yellow treasure in the tucks of her shirt. At first, I'm afraid she's going to get upset again. It is Mom's. Maybe I've pushed things too far. Maybe I—

"Thank you," Clara murmurs, picking it up and nestling it in the palm of her hand. "It's pretty."

The movie comes back on, and I take a quilt from the back of the couch and throw it across our laps. Not long after, my eyes drift shut. I will always remember this trip, this moment. Which is what Mom wanted. There is no place like home. Forever.

Tidings
Day Three

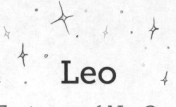

Leo

Fortress of No One but Me and Mom

It's a few minutes after sunrise. We're scattering across the beach, loading tidings into our wagons. All except Mom. Dad said she got up earlier than any of us this morning to run some errands in town. Not much is open this early, and Mom never misses a morning collection, but Dad said she'd meet us on the beach. She'll probably be as surprised and awed as I am to see the twins focused on their job today, loading their own wagon with a new sense of care like they'd grown up some overnight. There is really hope for them.

The sun's glinting on the ocean. It almost seems like yesterday's storm never happened, except the *Buoyant* rests near the dunes, oars by its side. I need to ask Dad to help me haul it to the garage later. I'm not sure when I'll get to take it out again or if I'll ever want to, but I can't leave it in the sand. Not after it brought me and Alice home.

I unwrap seaweed from a square tea tin and put the tin into my nearly full red wagon. I'm almost to the rocky part of the beach, and I haven't found anything from Gumpa yet. Every lid gives me a false spark of hope before I realize it's not another coffee can.

"Go ahead, Leo," Dad says, from not too far away. "With that rain yesterday, better check the tide pools."

Leaving the wagon, I leap across the first set of boulders, then vault from one rock to another. Since I know the footholds, I pause often, making sure to search the hidden pockets for some stray tidings. There are only sand crabs, some chipped shells, small pieces of driftwood. The niche where the Fortress hides is only a few rocks away.

A voice carries over the rush of water.

The ocean will show you the power of patience and time, if you let it.

That sounds an awful lot like Gumpa. Coming from the Fortress.

The power of patience and time.

I freeze. What's going on? Gumpa can't be here, can he? I mean, Alice did see her mom somehow, but . . .

I glance back at my dad, who waves. "I'm going a little farther," I call, and to my surprise, he gives me a thumbs-up.

I slip down into the hole and into the Fortress, my hands and feet skidding across the slippery rocks. As my eyes adjust to the dim light of the cave, I scuttle against the wall, nearly springing out of my skin. Someone's sitting cross-legged on the ledge. Someone in a purple bathing suit and floppy red hat, in the glow of one of my battery-operated lanterns.

"Mom?"

She definitely senses my huge disappointment and shock because she lifts a hand, her expression part-hello, part-apologetic. A brand-new, shiny tape player is tucked in her lap, the coffee can Gumpa sent me near her knees. A bunch of other stuff—a bottle of vegetable oil, a screwdriver, Q-tips, and another cassette tape—is spread out on a beach towel nearby. "Hi, Leo."

"How did you—this is my—why are—what are you—" Every question seems equally important. Mom is *in my Fortress.*

"Gumpa shared this place with me when I was your age."

My head's spinning. "So you still come here?"

"No, I haven't for a long time." She pats the shelf for me to join her, so I climb up. "I wanted this to be a special place for you and Gumpa, so when we moved in with him, I told him to share it with you. He loved hanging out here with you."

I settle against the wall. "I heard Gumpa's voice when I was on the rocks."

"I've been working on a surprise." She taps the cassette player with her finger. "I've been testing to see if I could make the tape any clearer."

"You can do that?"

"Back in the olden days, I may or may not have learned some tricks after spilling sodas on my own cassette player." She grins. "Want to listen? I didn't get every word, though, so don't get too excited."

She hits PLAY. There's a waterfall of static. Then—

Leo? It's Gumpa. By some miracle of current, this old tape found me again. Imagine my [chkshhh]. I'm afraid recording this might not work. But I must try to [phht-t-t-t]. I need you to get this to the Jones family. They should have it [shhhhh-whrrr]. Anny Jones believed so much [chkchkchk] hope in death [zzhhhrrr]. I want her family to find comfort in this [krrrssshhh] preserved piece of her life. You're my second-in-command [tk-tk-tk-tk] trust you. It's taken me many years to learn that the ocean will show you the power of patience and time, if you let it.

"That's the most I've heard so far," Mom says, stopping the tape. "It's astounding."

"It is." I give Mom a side hug as tight as I can, my free arm around her middle, my head on her shoulder. I can't believe my mother managed to pull so much out of the tape after everything it's been through, after everywhere it's been. After everything I did to disappoint her. "Play it again."

She rewinds and replays. We hear the same thing.

I draw my knees up to my chest and rest my head on top. Otherwise, my heart might just thunk out onto the cold wet ground. "Think I did what Gumpa wanted me to do?"

"You mean scare the life out of us, risk my wrath, and sail headfirst into a squall? Ha ha." She pats my shoulder. "Leo, you were his second-in-command. You never let Gumpa down. You know very well, as he did, that I would have hemmed and hawed and asked a thousand different kinds of why."

"But I thought he might be in real trouble."

"In a way, he was. Coming to terms with Mrs. Jones's death pained him so much that it lasted years."

"How do you think he knew the Joneses would come here?"

Mom fiddles with the damp hair on my neck. "Your guess is as good as mine. In any case, if the Joneses had never traveled to Aviles, you could've easily sent them the recording."

She leans her head back against the cool, damp rock wall. I tilt my head next to hers. The stone behind us reverberates with the crash of waves outside.

"I'm glad I could help Gumpa, Mom, but where is he exactly?" I ask. Here in the Fortress, where Gumpa brought us both, it seems like the perfect time. "Where did he go when he died?"

"I wish I knew."

"Would you think I was hallucinating if I saw him?" I ask, thinking about Alice's mom but not wanting to spill a secret that isn't mine. "When I was out in the ocean? Not that I did . . . but what if?"

"Hearing his voice on tape and seeing him in person? I'd say you were doubly blessed and making all kinds of island history."

We're silent as the cave whistles with the tide and wind. For a second, I wish I had seen Gumpa, so I could tell Mom about it. But at least my mom, unlike Alice's, is right here with me.

"Thank you for everything," I say simply.

"Have you heard the saying *Whistle for the wind*?" she asks.

"Like when you're stuck on a calm sea, you can whistle and summon wind to fill your sail?"

"Yes, only you have to be careful—you might get a storm instead. Nevertheless, you should always try. Sound familiar?" Mom nudges my head gently with her own. "I may not fully accept your tactics yesterday, but you did the right thing helping Alice with her mom. And helping Gumpa. That's what the best lighthouse keepers do."

"You think I'll make a good one someday?"

"How about sooner?" She sits up and begins packing the tape player and her supplies into a beach bag. "As much as I like hanging out here with you, I promised your dad we wouldn't leave him high and dry for breakfast. Plus, I've got a list fifty miles long today, which includes logging in the tidings and organizing the delivery schedule. Think you're up to taking the lead on some tidings tasks this time?"

"By myself?" A frizzle of excitement streaks through me.

"I'll be there for moral support if you need it." She winks. "Gumpa gave you a ton of responsibility when you could hardly spell the word, and your dad and I failed to see how meaningful that was to you. We were thinking you could take care of the lantern. Turn it off each morning and make sure it's polished? Your brothers and sisters will still get a chance to turn it on, of course."

I tackle her with another hug, this one full-on. "Thanks, Mom."

"But our first priority today," she says, drawing away to slide off the shelf, "should be the Joneses. Not that fresh doughnuts can erase your boat ride with Alice, but we could go pick some up from town when the grocery store opens. They might be a nice way for the Joneses to wake up after yesterday. A peace offering. Plus, we don't want Mr. Jones to give a bad impression of us on his radio show."

"He'd do that?"

"Oh, I was only joking, Leo." Mom chuckles at what I'm sure is panic flashing across my face. "Mr. Jones wouldn't do anything like that."

I hop onto the ground next to her, dread rushing through me. "He was supposed to talk about our family—the lighthouse keepers. So is he gonna bring up Gumpa's tape? What if he does and thousands upon thousands of people tune in? If they find out about Alice's experience, will they rush down here, hunting for cassette tapes of their own?"

"I'm fairly certain Mr. Jones won't mention the tape. Something tells me he needs lots more time to wrap his head around all the things he's learned by being here."

I frown. "Could I take the doughnuts by? Talk to him about it?"

Mom eyes me hesitantly. I turn my frown into a toothy smiling *Please*.

"I did want you to give Alice these." She opens her beach bag and pulls out a bunch of envelopes fastened by an oversize paper clip. The return addresses are from Anny Jones. "I searched through Gumpa's boxes after you mentioned Alice's mom writing to him."

"I can do that," I say as she tucks them back into the bag for safekeeping. I can't wait to give them to Alice. "They're the letters that began everything."

We climb out of the Fortress, helping each other balance

on the rocks. "Promise to mind your manners when you see Mr. Jones," she says when we've found our footing. "That family has had quite the experiences on this island. And I promise that my invading your space here was a one-time thing."

"Deal." I jump onto the next rock and glance over my shoulder with a smile. "But I think it needs a new name. The Fortress of No One but Me and Mom."

Alice

What Have You Got to Lose?

When I wake up, Clara is stretched across me on the couch, her head on my stomach, mouth open. My first reaction is to wince at the drool, but my second is that it's nice to have her so close. Her hand is curled under her chin, and I can see the pink edges of Mom's shell tucked inside her palm. I don't dare move, even though her elbow's digging into my right leg. I smile. I don't think this is what Mom meant when she told me every second was a lifetime of love.

I glance around the living room, listening for Dad and Neesha. When my eyes land on the coffee table, I notice the TV is off and our cereal bowls are gone. There's a stream of sunlight and a note in Dad's handwriting.

Went to the beach for a short walk. Back for breakfast.
Love,
Dad & Neesha
P.S. Stay put.
P.S. #2. And be good.

I frown at the first P.S., knowing it will be a thousand years before they'll trust me to go anywhere again by myself. The second P.S. makes me wonder what they thought, seeing me and Clara, tangled up in each other's space willingly. That it definitely wouldn't last. Maybe that was the reason Dad and Neesha slipped out without a sound. They didn't want to break the spell, because they knew it would be broken eventually.

I'm not exactly rushing to test that theory out, but my arm's beginning to tingle. Somehow I'll need to move soon, or figure out how to wake Clara without sabotaging our renewed "sisterly love." So I'm grateful when the kitchen door rattles, the jingle and fit of a key in a lock. Neesha and Dad ease in, peeking our way.

"Anyone want breakfast?" Neesha calls softly when I wiggle my hand in a stiff greeting.

As if on cue, Clara yawns, blinks a few times, and sits up. She rubs her eyes. "Food?"

"You woke the beasts," Dad says, and I laugh, happy that he can joke after yesterday. I stretch and yawn, which prompts Neesha to yawn, too.

"Seems we all had a late night." Dad plunks down in the chair next to me. His hair's a mess from the sea breeze. "Guess you're used to the Wicked Witch of the West and her flying monkeys by now or you would've come in to get us."

"You knew we were up?" I ask. "Why didn't you say something?"

"Because you weren't yelling at each other." Neesha grins,

taking a spot on the floor between Dad and me. A little bit of sand clings to her bare legs. "We didn't want to jinx the situation."

"So why were you guys awake?" I ask.

"We were talking," Dad answers. "About everything that's happened since we got here to the island. About the radio show. About our family."

"Did you change your minds?" Clara bounces on the couch. "Are you gonna get married?"

Neesha flashes a soft, knowing smile at my dad. "We did discuss that, but not yet. Someday. When we're home and ready and you can properly ask me. Together."

She flutters her eyelashes and makes kissy lips at Dad, which makes us giggle. Even though his cheeks and forehead are red from the sun, I know he's blushing.

"Wait." Clara cuts into the moment. "You're not thinking we should go back to Maryland early, are you? Because of Leo and Alice?"

My smile vanishes, and I glance at Dad for confirmation.

"We're not going home early," he reassures us. "There's a little more story for me to tie up here. We need some more family time, too."

"What is your story now, Dad?" I ask, relieved that we're staying on Aviles a little longer and very curious about what parts my dad has to "tie up."

"After an intense few days," he says, "I think we need to figure that out together."

"Then let's eat," Clara declares, so Dad and Neesha yank

us both off the couch in a flurry of arms and legs. Everyone's so happy. I'm holding my breath that it lasts.

As we crowd into the galley kitchen, there's a knock at the door. Neesha leans around the fridge to get a glimpse of who it is. "Is that Leo Mercury?"

I glance down at my faded, stretched-out purple T-shirt and shorts that I never wear in public, but offer to open the door anyway. Pajamas shouldn't matter when you've tackled a tsunami with someone.

When I say hi, Leo holds out a white-and-pink-striped box. I get a whiff of butter, sugar, cinnamon, and goodness. Doughnuts. "Mom and I got these fresh from town and thought you'd enjoy them," he explains.

Clara says hello to him, reaches around me, and claims the box.

"Don't be rude, Clara," Neesha clucks from behind us, and invites Leo inside. Dad's already getting plates and a pitcher of water.

"I wanted to apologize again for yesterday." Leo finds a spot to stand out of the way, just outside the kitchen door. He squirms with the strap of his backpack, slung across his shoulders. "It wasn't Alice who wanted to go out in the boat. I convinced her to. And it might've seemed careless, but I did have good intentions."

Before I can prevent him from taking my share of the blame, Leo launches into a speech I'm almost sure he practiced more than once on the way over. Dad and Neesha have forgotten breakfast and lean against the counter. Clara's not paying much attention, wolfing down a cruller.

"And after Alice told me about wanting to contact her mom," he says in a breathless rush, a bead of sweat trickling down the side of his face, "everything fell into place."

"He was helping me, Dad," I tack on, when I sense an opening, "but I was helping him just as much. We were both helping his grandfather, too."

"Gumpa wanted to make sure your family got the interview," Leo says. "To remember her by."

Dad straightens up. The kitchen suddenly seems as small as a matchbox.

"Your intentions were good at heart, Leo," he says, his tone unexpectedly sympathetic, "and so were yours, Alice. And this entire story is mind-blowing. But it'll take me a long, long time, most likely never, ever, to get over what happened with you both in that boat. I'm a dad. That's how I'm supposed to feel."

Easing up a little with my dad's reassuring smile, Leo knuckles the sweat from his forehead. "There's one other thing, Mr. Jones. I'm worried about your show even more than I was before. My grandfather said people who learn about the tidings will turn this place upside-down expecting their own miracles. Since he's not around to prevent that, I have to. And if you tell your listeners about the cassette tape he sent me and Alice, I won't ever be able to stop them from coming."

"You're not going to talk about the cassette tape, are you, Dad?" I ask. "You haven't even listened to it yourself."

With a gracious nudge, Neesha suggests we go to the dining table to continue the conversation. Clara brings the doughnuts and plates. Dad sits across from me and Leo, with Neesha and Clara taking the ends.

"This island is extraordinary to say the least." Dad puts his elbows on the table. "It'll take me years to reflect on our experience here. But I can tell you one thing: I will only share what your family wishes me to share, and I will never do anything to jeopardize the unique traditions of your community. In fact, I'd like you and your family to personally help me shape the story for my show. Make sure I get it right."

"Seriously?"

"Seriously," Dad replies. "I'd like to get your angle."

Leo beams, obviously happy about my dad's invitation. Then he glances at the clock above the table. "Mom's letting me sort and deliver the tidings collection so I have to get going. But she said you could come over for dinner tonight—if you don't mind spending more time in a household hurricane. Dad added that."

Grinning at Mr. Mercury's comment, Neesha and Dad agree to dinner, and I walk Leo outside to the bike he left near the driveway. He takes off his backpack, unzips the main pocket, and hands me a bundle of letters. "I also wanted to give you these. Mom found them in Gumpa's files. They're from your mom."

"Wow." I trace my mom's handwriting across the first envelope. "I'll keep them with the ones from your grandfather. Somewhere extra-special."

But when I think about Mom's work strewn across my bedroom floor back home in Maryland, the piles seem far from special. Maybe Neesha and Dad can help me sort through them. Clara, too, if she wants.

"My mom fixed Gumpa's side of the tape some," Leo notes before I can do something weird like thank him with a hug. He hurls the backpack across his shoulders and climbs onto his bike. "She's working on the interview next. When you come over, you can play it for your dad. So he can understand better."

"I'd like to."

Leo's about to push off when he says, "Thanks for sticking up for me in there."

"Thanks for coming to talk with my dad and Neesha."

Leo pedals away, calling out that he'll see us later. When I rejoin the ruckus in the kitchen, Neesha's supervising as Clara makes scrambled eggs. I go hang out with Dad, who stayed at the table. I sit next to him and put Mom's letters off to the side.

"By the way, you're never leaving my sight for the next decade," he says. "I only went for a walk on the beach this morning because Neesha convinced me you'd be okay."

"Maybe you need to talk with Dr. Figg about that," I joke, feeling like I truly can.

"Maybe we can talk to her together," he replies, to my surprise. "Really talk. I think my feelings have been on mute awhile, too."

I picture us at Dr. Figg's, me without markers and paper, expressing how I feel with actual, spoken words. It would be life-changing if I didn't have to worry about losing my voice anymore, if what happened here on Aviles Island, and on the boat with Leo, somehow helped me get past it. And with Dad there with me, maybe what I want to say won't disappear into the beige wallpaper anymore.

Then again, Dad's here. Now.

"I'd like that," I say, laying my head on his shoulder. "But we could talk before then, too. I'd like to tell you what happened out in the ocean. I'd like to talk about finding Mom."

"Me too." Dad takes my hand and folds it in his. He tilts his chin slightly toward the end of the table where I set the letters. "So, what are those?"

"Leo brought them," I reply, snuggling farther into him. His shirt smells like sun and salt. "More for us to talk about."

My heart is full when he touches his head to mine. In trying to find my mom, I found my dad.

Leo

The Light of Life

The sun's halfway down. We ate dinner on the beach behind the lighthouse: the Joneses on a big flowered sheet, and my family on two holey bedspreads littered with wet beach towels.

Now Alice and I sit side by side in the *Buoyant*, landlocked where we left it yesterday. Her damp hair is riddled with sand from the cartwheel competition we had earlier with Willa, Clara, and Vivien. My own hair feels stiff, like it belongs on one of Willa's hand-me-down-from-Viv Barbies.

"This thing was a lot stronger than it looks," Alice says, working her fingernail against a sliver of peeling paint. "Seaworthy and then some."

"Told you," I say. She punches my arm lightly, and I grin. "But Gumpa did name it the *Buoyant*."

"My mom had something in her notes about boat names." Alice wrinkles her nose as if that will help her remember. "Something like, giving a boat the wrong name is the difference between good luck and being lost at sea."

"Guess Gumpa chose the right name."

She nods. "Do you think you'll get a message back from him?"

I tell her about searching the beach this morning and not finding anything. "I'd at least like to know if he's all right with the way things turned out. Like me meeting you and your family."

Alice gazes down the beach toward the rocks, slightly glowing from the slant of the sun. "From what you've told me about your grandfather, I bet he'd say this would make a great story one day."

I totally agree.

"Time to light the lantern!" Mom calls from the family compound. "Who wants to come?"

Alice and I scramble out of the boat. After the hubbub of folding blankets and collecting sand toys, we follow the troops up the dunes to the lighthouse to hose down.

"Leo," Dad says from somewhere in the middle of the crowd as we move inside the house, "why don't you lead Alice and her family up first?"

"Watch your step," I warn them, and we climb single file up the staircase into the lantern room. Mr. Jones, Neesha, and Clara immediately go to the windows. They ooh and aah over the ocean, which looks like smooth purple glass glazed with gold. Clara's showing Neesha some kind of shell and lifting it up like it belongs against the sunset. A few seagulls fly past, their shapes shadowy against the sky.

"Leo," Mom calls from the steps, "you and Alice can flip the switch."

I let Alice into the control room ahead of me. Her face is bright with the biggest smile I've ever seen. "My mom used to say that it's the lighthouse keeper's job to shine light across the waves so no one ever gets lost or forgotten. I'll never forget you, Leo Mercury."

"I won't forget you either, Alice Jones." I smile. "We could write letters back and forth, even though snail mail takes forever?"

"That would be perfect," she says. "Our own version of the tidings!"

We agree to make it happen, then I ask if she's ready to turn on the lantern. With our hands side by side, we hit the switch. The light rolls across the darkening ocean.

Alice and I stand next to her family at the windows. My brothers and sisters and my parents squeeze in behind us. Shoulder to shoulder, as we watch the light pan to the north, I see a glow on the horizon. It's almost as if another lantern is flashing, far away in some there-not-there place, signaling that love shines bright enough across space and time to guide people home.

Acknowledgments

I promised my daughter, Sophie, that I would thank her first. She read a hundred drafts of this story, brainstormed ideas, became indignant over certain edits, answered my many questions, and always offered thoughtful critical comments. She's my dreamer, my cheerleader, my public relations guru, my fashion consultant, and my daily reminder of everything beautiful, fun, and full of love. *Mommy loves you.*

I owe a million hot and cold beverages to my writing group: Rachel Owens, Dustin Weeks, Bryan Seagrave, Chris Gebhardt, Maggie Karda, Michael Flota, and Jennifer Russi. They've read nearly every single word of this book, in its multitude of forms. They've watched me think, scribble, type, revise, and try to plot. If there was a superhero team of writers, they would be it. Every one of you is awesome.

I bestow the title of Executive Dream-Maker to my agent, Taylor Martindale Kean of Full Circle Literary Agency. From our first phone call, I have been beyond grateful to be part of her magic. Her keen eye, enthusiasm, and constant positivity inspire my creativity and keep me going on the long road to publication. Writers always talk about finding "that one special person out there" who will love your voice. I thank my lucky stars that Taylor took a chance on those very first pages I sent her.

The sparkle in this novel comes from my brilliant, talented editors at FSG: Janine O'Malley, and her assistant, Melissa Warten. Their confidence in this story, their thoughtful brainstorming, and their expertise in the publishing field were invaluable in shaping not only Alice and Leo's adventure, but mine as well. They, along with the help of an amazing team, made sure this book gleamed. Thank you to cover artist Dion MBD and designer Trisha Previte, who captured the essence of the novel with starry imagination. Thank you to copy editor Chandra Wohleber, as well as production editors Taylor Pitts and Ilana Worrell, who can suggest one word and it transforms an entire scene. And thank you to Brittany Pearlman and Leigh Ann Higgins, the publicists in charge of introducing this book to fantastic readers everywhere.

There are countless other people who have followed along in my journey as a writer. My dearest friend, Heather Eaton, read early drafts, kept me fed, lathered me in love, shared in my hopes, and offered so many hugs. My sister, Susan Ground, offered her endless affirmation, editorial wisdom, and astute feedback. My mom, Linda Stoddard, who reads books by the stack, fostered my love of reading before I was even in preschool and sparked my lifelong interest in words. *I love you, Mom.* My siblings, Eric and Kim Stoddard, always knew that writing was my calling and had faith that my childhood scribbles would amount to something meaningful. Frank Gunshanan, Rich Vollaro, and my other stellar colleagues at Daytona State College cheered me on with every published poem and every story.

To you, the readers, I give my endless gratitude and appreciation for spending your precious time with Leo and Alice on Aviles Island. When I wrote this book, I thought often about how I could transport you to a place of hope and miracles, even for a minute. With every story I write, you make me imagine how impossibility can become possibility.

And there are never enough words to thank my husband, Charles. For thirty-one years, through mellow tides and challenging seas, he has been my foundation, my constant, and my compass. He is my partner, my teacher, my role model, my husband, my best friend, and an incredible father to our girl. He teaches me how to face fears and encourages me to live up to my fullest potential. His love is boundless. He will forever be my lighthouse. He will forever be my way home. With everything he has done to support me, this is his book as much as mine. *You always knew I could do this. I love you so very much. Happily ever after.*